Kensington books by Jodi Thomas

Someday Valley Novels
Strawberry Lane
The Wild Lavender Bookshop

Honey Creek Novels
Breakfast at the Honey Creek Café
Picnic in Someday Valley
Dinner on Primrose Hill
Sunday at the Sunflower Inn

Historical Romance
Beneath the Texas Sky

Anthologies
The Wishing Quilt
A Texas Kind of Christmas
The Cowboy Who Saved Christmas
Be My Texas Valentine
Give Me a Cowboy
Give Me a Texan
Give Me a Texas Outlaw
Give Me a Texas Ranger
One Texas Night
A Texas Christmas

The
Wild
Lavender
Bookshop

JODI
THOMAS

ZEBRA BOOKS
Kensington Publishing Corp.
www.kensingtonbooks.com

For the love of my life

Prologue

Autumn in the Valley

Andi Delane drove into Honey Creek, Texas, tired, hungry, and driving way over the speed limit as usual. With the windows down, she felt as if she was in her Cessna with the wind streaming by and not a care in the world. If only that were true.

When she was a kid, she loved Easter egg hunts and she still enjoyed searching, solving puzzles, and digging up the truth now and then. Today she was waiting at the starting line. Studying the lay of the land. Mapping out her route. Guessing where the best hiding places were on this unknown region of Texas just as she would if she were going to go back undercover. When she was six years old, she told her mother she wanted to live full speed, and it never occurred to her in all the years since to slow down.

A screaming police siren blared behind her, ruining her thoughts of flying. Maybe at thirty-two she should stop dreaming of Easter egg hunts and try watching the rearview mirror once in a while.

She pulled into mud leftover from a dawn dusting of snow.

The cool air made her eyes water as she stepped out of the Jeep. She hated the cold and the wind, and in Texas it was always blowing.

Suddenly she was shaded by a silhouette of a very big trooper. Six feet six or more, she'd guess. His features were shaded by his hat. County deputy sheriff's badge at eye level to her, service weapon on his side, and an electronic ticket device in hand.

Andi faced him straight on as she wiped her watery eyes. "You just ruined a great adventure I was having. I was on a hunt until the morning cold hit my face."

The cop was maybe late twenties, hard to tell from this viewpoint. His smile turned to a frown. "I hate to make your day worse, ma'am. Please don't cry but you really do need to pay attention to your driving. I'm afraid I'm going to have to give you a ticket."

She thought of telling him she usually traveled at 100 mph on back roads, or she could pull out her badge. But this trip was personal, not work. Instead, she showed him her driver's license. She remained silent. Nothing else. He didn't have to know why she was in Honey Creek. This trip she wanted to be invisible. In and out of town. All she had to do was find the brothers some lawyer said she had. If they were no-good hicks or men no one would want for kin, she'd head out leaving nothing but skid marks and dust in her path. The lawyer would know where they lived.

Once she met them, she'd look around the town she was born in, take a few pictures and stay a few days just to rest, away from Dallas and her problems there.

The big deputy handed her the ticket and said, "Now you drive safe and have a great day in our beautiful town, Miss Andi Delane."

She remembered what her pop said, *Always be polite to the*

law but don't tell them any more than you have to. They'll forget you faster.

"Good day, Deputy." She never looked back as she headed out. Within a mile she saw her destination: the little town of Honey Creek. She tossed the ticket out the window and forgot the deputy.

Andi circled the town twice before she saw the lawyer's name on a second-story window. Jackson Landry had called her mother, who passed on Andi's very private number. He'd said that Andi was named in a will in Honey Creek. The only place she'd even seen that town's name was on her birth certificate. The whole thing sounded interesting, but she had a few questions first.

Deputy Danny Davis watched the ticket he'd just written dance in the wind. He had the urge to grab it, chase her down and return it to her along with a citation for littering.

He shook his head. The lady had fire in her eyes. He hadn't really looked at a woman since his college love stomped on his heart. He'd cried like a baby when he found his engagement ring taped to the dash of his pickup. And, believe it or not, no one wants to see a football lineman cry.

Almost eight years since, Danny convinced himself he didn't even care if women noticed him or not. However, today might be an exception. Andi Delane was a woman no man could overlook.

He'd probably never see her again but, man, he'd love to see those eyes. He bet they'd flash pure fire when she was angry and sparkle like the sun when she laughed.

Danny said to himself, "If any man ever got close enough."

Chapter 1

Noah's Contentment

Monday

Noah O'Brien stepped out of his bookshop to greet the first light of dawn rising over the main street of Honey Creek. He dusted off the little red tables and chairs he'd set out front for the sunrise coffee drinkers.

Of course, he had chairs inside along the windows for reading with a cup in hand, but there was something special about watching the day start.

"Another day in paradise," he thought. Let the rest of the people in the world hurry about and argue and plan for a better life. He'd found contentment here at thirty-three years old in this Texas valley.

Three little towns were nestled between farms and ranches. Honey Creek, the county seat. Clifton Bend, a college town full of ideas and energy. And then his favorite, Someday Valley, which was almost a town. Honey Creek was organized, cute. Clifton was a beehive, busy, while shacks were scattered like marbles among the rocky land of Someday Valley.

On his day off he sometimes circled the valley. He lived in Honey Creek, often went to lectures at Clifton Bend, but he relaxed when he drove through Someday Valley.

It was an interesting mix of locations, all within shouting distance. Honey Creek, the biggest of the towns, gave that proper small-town feel and was settled by families who wanted the small-town lifestyle. Clifton Bend was full of youth, dreams, and laughter and was originally settled by artists and creatives whose spirits still infused the place. Someday Valley, in contrast, was first inhabited by fishermen. Salt of the earth with a great work ethic and independent mindset. The valley still smelled of fish, beer, and time, as if history dwelt there. An eclectic smattering of people for sure, but Noah thought somehow the towns fit together.

Noah stared at the town square lined in old elms covered in autumn leaves.

"My valley, my home, my life," he whispered. There was balance in the world here, Noah thought. An order that settled his soul.

As he prepared the shop for morning customers, he smiled at the view out his bookshop windows. The big county courthouse watched over the park on one side. Half a dozen tiny stores faced the square from another side. This strip of brightly colored awnings shaded an ice cream parlor, a café, a great bakery that sweetened the dawn air, and a flower shop that accidentally gave Noah the idea for the name of his store. Wild Lavender Bookshop.

On the far side of the square stood a lonely two-pump gas station run by three brothers. Old tires formed a fortress around it. As far as Noah knew, the gas pumps never closed. The decrepit station was banked by vacant lots, usually empty except for a few wrecked pickups that had been parked there since the nineties. The owners never came back to get them. The rusty old trucks had morphed into almost art. No matter what time of day or night, one of the Edwards brothers was sleeping in a wooden rocker in the shade of their DOWN TOWN EXXON sign.

The last side of the square block was Noah's favorite. It was his nest. One long three-story building of red brick stood against the wind off the creek. The bookshop and a few other stores were on the first floor and above were apartments. No matter what window he looked out of, he saw a peaceful view. The town square shined from the front of the building, with manicured walks between the trees and benches. But from Noah's back windows he saw the creek that had broken off from the Brazos River that wiggled over eight hundred miles across Texas.

The locals liked to say that the stream splashed and waved as it flowed. Some folks claimed the water giggled now and then as it passed.

The three-story building Noah lived and worked in was called "Bear's Mall." Everyone called the big man who owned it Bear. He ran a repair shop that shared Noah's south bookstore wall. All was quiet when Bear was gone farming, but when he was open, noise always drifted through. Folks said Bear Buchanan didn't live; he just worked.

On the ends of the first floor of the mall were Sandy's Beauty Shop and Kandy's Card Shop. Sandy never stopped talking, Kandy never stopped laughing, and Bear never stopped running when he saw them coming in his direction.

When Noah moved into one of the old, dilapidated apartments above the businesses, the rent was right and Bear was usually there to help if something broke.

Noah's roomy bookstore smelled of mahogany and coffee, and when the door opened, a hint of lavender. A simple sign hung above the door: TRAVEL BETWEEN THE COVERS. Ordinary posters of book covers through the ages were taped to the wall and a cash register rattled and bumped his stomach every time it opened.

No colorful displays in the windows to catch the interest of folks walking by. The second floor was the same. Plain apartments with long windows and floors that creaked. There was a third floor on the mall; it was cluttered and dark. The owner claimed the ghosts of the first pioneers rested up there and secrets were hidden beneath the dust.

Almost three years ago, Noah O'Brien had driven into Honey Creek and decided to stay. Being an only child, he'd been pushed by his parents since he came out of the womb. He learned to read by four, played every sport, made straight A's, got into the best college, worked to climb the ladder of success and still wasn't happy. He even bought a starter house, intending to move up every five years according to some nameless, faceless plan that meant nothing to him.

He'd played their game until, on his thirtieth birthday, he just couldn't do it anymore. Or in his parents' words, *lost his mind*. He quit his boring IT job, sold that starter house he hated, emptied all his bank accounts, packed his car, and ran away from his life. Then he drove around the country until he found where he wanted to live.

On his second day in Honey Creek, he wandered into a dusty old bookstore. When he noticed a faded FOR LEASE sign, he knew this was that place.

Noah cleaned up the old store, kept the dusty books, and bought more inventory. He learned to make great coffee for a buck a cup. He bought sweets from the bakery a block over and sold them at cost. Then at dusk, he would lock up and feed the leftover scones to the ducks while walking the river's bank.

Within a month he knew he'd found paradise.

His favorite thing to do in this little town was listen to the locals' conversations. At first, he was just trying to understand the Texans' accent. But, between the gossip and "what was wrong with the government," they talked of what they wished they'd done.

Noah could almost see sorrow behind aged, watery eyes as

they told of adventures they'd only read about, paths they'd never walked, choices they'd never made.

In the big cities Noah noticed people talked of what they planned to do or listed what they'd accomplished, but here they talked of what they'd never gotten around to doing.

Sometimes he looked behind their wizened expressions and imagined the goals and untraveled roads, the love affairs they hadn't risked, and the fears they never revealed. The customers who walked down the aisles of his shop seemed to be looking for something. An adventure? Some secret they might find? Maybe a road map to another life?

Noah promised himself that when his time came, he'd have no "wish I'd done" list.

Once in a while he caught a spark of excitement in people's rambling, and sometimes that longing stared back from the mirror. He was proud he'd left home to live his own dreams, but had he gone far enough?

The mailman tapped a handful of mail on the open doorframe and brought Noah out of his thoughts. "Morning, Noah."

Noah grinned. "Morning, Tim, how is business?"

"Fine. Running late getting started. Everyone seems to stop me and talk."

Sealing his lips, Noah waved goodbye.

Noah looked over the mail. The first two envelopes were bills and the last one was handwritten to him from New York.

He tossed it into the trash without opening.

The mailman said from the doorway, "I thought that one might be important."

"No, my parents' attorney writes now and then like he's one of the family," Noah said, more to himself than to the mailman. "The first year I left New York they begged me to come home where I belong. Second year they tried to demand it, and lately they've been threatening me. But I'm not leaving. I love it here. It makes me smile when someone wanders into the stacks and now and then finds just what they are looking for. A good story, or a tender tale that makes them cry, or dark stories that make them afraid. Whatever they read, they feel more alive and a smile drifts over them."

But best of all, he listened and watched as they learned. Noah loved hearing his visitors say, *If I could only do . . .* They had desire hiding inside for bigger bites of life, but the courage to make any changes seemed dried up.

Sometimes they'd admit they were content in feeling safe. All Noah could do was wish with them. Slowly he was learning the difference between a goal and a dream. Each had its place.

He was a mute cheerleader, silently yelling from the stands.

Some of Honey Creek's residents were living in heaven and others wished they could run away. Heaven seemed to have a different address for each.

Every night Noah climbed to the roof of his apartment two flights above the bookshop and wrote down the conversations he had heard. He'd log what they might become one day because of the books he had encouraged them to read. He'd see a smile after they'd encountered adventure between the covers of a book.

He'd never wanted to be a mind reader or a fortune teller, helping folks find their way. He simply wanted to walk invisibly among them and observe. He knew he was one of those people who watched life unfold, yet never got into the game.

"I'll write about a town where individuals long to live their dreams," he thought, "knowing if they don't, they will become mindless chatterers drinking coffee and nothing more."

They'd be like Bear's daughters, who came in every Wednesday to have coffee and complain about their father getting older. Noah mentally corrected his thought. Katherine complained. Cora Lee, the younger daughter, usually just nodded.

The question he'd try to figure out would whisper inside him, *Would they be happier if Bear Buchanan changed his life?*

Would it matter or would they just find something else to complain about? Was it even about Bear at all, or just how they communicated as sisters with nothing more in common than their father?

Bear had inherited the strip mall when he came home from the Army. He was also a farmer who talked of his crops from spring to fall. The man who folks said never stopped working seemed to be happy. When he was in his workshop, Noah often heard him whistling.

Noah pondered over his wild thoughts when the first people hurried in just as the coffee was ready. They doctored their cups with sugar and cream, then rushed to the red chairs outside.

If Noah ever shared his theories on life with this crowd, they'd think him insane. If he said nothing, no one would notice or change. Life would just move on as it always had. Dreams were dreams, and life was reality that rolled over them; words and ideas didn't really matter.

Noah knew that he was simply a tall, thin bookstore owner who had no goals, no lovers, and not one dream. A constant watcher more out of habit than desire.

Until one day, Noah decided he'd become a writer. Then he'd live, he told himself. He'd ride the wind as Steinbeck did or enjoy adventure as Hemingway did when he fought in faraway wars. He would create worlds like George Orwell or push the boundaries as J. D. Salinger had.

Noah almost laughed. Salinger said he wasn't like the people around him.

"I'm not either," Noah said to himself.

His voice rose. "I'm not wasting time. I'm incubating a dozen ideas, then I'll live my dreams, soon."

The moment his words died, Noah thought he heard laughter, but when he turned around no one was there.

"Probably a visiting ghost from the third floor." He gazed at the empty aisles. "You know, I don't believe in ghosts so just go on back to the third floor where everyone claims all the ghosts hang out." He smiled. "Haven't you ever heard of 'ghosting' someone?"

Suddenly Harry Pratt darted through the door, waving his cane like a sword. "Mr. O'Brien, take this crime down before I forget the facts!"

"Got it, Harry, but maybe you should walk down the street and tell the sheriff."

Harry raised his voice. "I might forget a detail. There is no time to waste. Write the facts down!"

Harry paced as he started. "I, Harry Pratt, swear I saw a crime committed on Main Street today." He looked at his watch. "At nine twenty today, sharp."

Noah held up a pen. "Harry, you said *today* twice."

"Then mark one out, Noah."

"Which one?"

"I don't care. I'm trying to report a crime."

Noah tried to look serious. "What did Earl do this time?"

"He scratched a car parked right on Main with the oldest printer I've ever seen."

"Maybe you should tell the sheriff or one of the deputies."

Harry frowned. "The sheriff said to report any crimes to you if his car wasn't out front of the station."

"What!!! I'm not a cop."

Harry yelled back, "Sheriff Pecos said he'd deputize you if you want him to. He said my writing looks like a first-grader who's failing ancient Greek."

Noah gave in. "All right, Harry. Give me the details. What car did he scratch?"

Harry cleared his throat and prepared to testify. "Earl scratched a blue Ford parked in front of your store. A 1988. Big scratch, worse than the one he made last year with his toaster on the roof of the same car."

"What?" Noah lowered his voice. "Are you telling me Earl dropped his own printer and scratched his own car?"

"Toaster last year and printer today. It won't be long till he's parking junk cars on the street."

Noah figured if he could act calm for the next minute he should move to Hollywood and become an actor. He felt laughter all the way to his toes.

"I've got the facts, Harry. I'll type them up and get the report right to Pecos. Thank you for your service."

An hour later Noah emailed a very detailed three-page report.

The sheriff responded almost immediately. THANKS.

Noah smiled. He knew that one-word reply contained lots of snark, and he wasn't sorry he caused it. If the sheriff insisted on dragging Noah into this game, he'd play.

Ball's in your court, Barney Fife.

Chapter 2

Bear's Emergency

Monday

Bart "Bear" Buchanan locked his repair shop on Main and headed out before his two daughters showed up to take him to lunch. Whenever his oldest, Katherine, wanted money, or needed anything from him, she always fed him first. His youngest, Cora, got dragged along for the event just like he did, because if there was anything Katherine loved it was an audience. While Katherine insisted on pretending she was concerned about his health, what she was really concerned about was his bank account, and right now he cared more about finding a very large cheeseburger than listening to her whine.

"Morning, Bear," Noah shouted from the bookshop entry as he stepped toward the tiny tables. The bookshop owner set little bud vases with a bit of lavender on each table. "You headed out for an early lunch or would you like a cup of coffee this morning?"

Bart, who everyone in town called Bear, growled at the question, but he managed a one-sided smile. He knew he was a size bigger than most folks, with hands rough and scarred and more powerful than a man half his age. Some said his hands should be registered as weapons, but Bear just grinned as he waved at Noah O'Brien. The bookworm might be shy and a few months overdue for a haircut, but Bear saw him as an old soul. He was interesting, yet cautious. As if he wanted to sink into the woodwork rather than be noticed.

Bear slowed to talk to the kid and no matter how busy he was, he put in the effort to connect on some level. He'd learned years ago if you take the time to talk about nothing, a neighbor will be around when you need him.

"Nope, no coffee, Noah. Not even an early lunch. I've got to go pick up a broken refrigerator out on West Road. May take a while. I'll try to fix it out at the farm so I won't have to haul it in. If anyone needs me, have them leave a note and I'll call them when I can."

"Will do, Bear," Noah said as he stepped back into the bookshop.

Bear frowned at the young man's back. Someday he'd tell Noah to stop calling him Bear. That had been his nickname when he was a mechanic in the Army overseas. He had figured he'd go back to his rightful name once he mustered out, but somehow "Bear" stuck.

He growled again. That first year home, he'd lost his real name and his wife. Oh, she didn't die, she just ran back to Germany and never returned. Bear had been in his early thirties like Noah was now, only he had two girls to raise. He wanted to work on engines, and his parents wanted him to farm. The only answer was to do both.

Three years ago, Noah O'Brien moved in next door to him. He was renting both the bookshop and one of the apartments upstairs. While Bear thought Noah was a nice guy, they had nothing in common. Most days they couldn't keep a conversation going long enough to finish a cup of coffee. Bear was now in his late fifties, had served eight years in the Army, then came home a changed man, somehow broken, a loner.

Noah was the opposite. He had run away from home somewhere back east. Noah might be in his early thirties and talk a bit funny, but to Bear he was still wet behind the ears. A quiet man who seemed afraid to dive into life.

Between his farm and the repair shop, Bear worked most days somewhere, while Noah was just reading books every time Bear saw him.

"Maybe that's his work." He shrugged.

Noah rushed back to the doorway. "If your daughters ask where you are, what should I say?"

Bear fought down a few cusswords that were hanging on his tongue. "I'll be out at Holly Rim."

Noah said what everyone always said: "Holly Rim. Don't get lost. I hear folks who go too close to the valley's rim on that farm, get turned around and never make it back."

Before Bear answered, the kid disappeared back inside like a cuckoo clock. For once Bear had told the truth—a truth that would even hold his daughters at bay. He rushed to his pickup, suddenly in a hurry to leave town. He didn't want to talk to anyone. He just wanted to drive to Holly Rim, where legends moved among the trees.

Deep in the rocky hills that formed the rim of the valley lay a rugged plot of land that one family had owned since the first settlers came to this part of Texas. A tale was told by the Apache, who'd traveled through the valley from their winter campsite to their summer hunting grounds. They said that sorrow walked among the uneven paths, and thorny holly grew as tall as trees on the west rim. Rain washed away the paths, and winds cut more trails as if to confuse strangers. Several tried to climb to the rim in the early days, but few did today. And some who went in, never came out. Forever lost in the winding paths and rocky cliffs.

He drove ten miles over the speed limit to get to one of the oldest homesteads in the county and he planned to take his time fixing anything Eliza Dosela needed fixing.

Bear Buchanan knew the legend well. His people had settled just below Eliza's place near the ridge. All below Holly Rim was farmland as tranquil as the rim was wild. At the break in between the two landscapes, one lonely house stood.

He was in his teens when he first saw her. She was running near the fence. Her midnight hair flew in the wind like a cape. She was so small he thought she was a fairy for a moment.

Over time, Bear watched for her just so he could wave. It took weeks but finally one day, she waved back.

Eliza wasn't yet in high school when he left for the Army. To his surprise, she was sitting on her gate by the road when he drove past on his way to boot camp. Both skinny arms were waving wildly as he slowed and yelled, "I'll be back."

Bear remembered feeling a loss for something he'd never really had as he watched her run on the other side of the fence. He liked to think she'd been waiting to wave goodbye.

He'd remembered her as more fairy than girl. When Bear had been in the Army, the thought of her kept him going when there was danger. His imagined his very own fairy watched over him from Texas. He'd never said her name out loud but she meant something to him.

One house a mile from his farm he knew nothing about. One girl innocent and free as he so longed to be. One memory that carried him through the worst the Army had to offer and brought him back to a place both mysterious and wild in his imagination.

Bear didn't talk to her when he came home, but he waved when he passed her place and she waved back. For a while she was nothing more than a mystery. He heard her folks died while he'd been gone, but he probably wouldn't have been welcome at the graveside funeral. Folks said she stood alone by her parents' graves.

When Bear's life had weathered to endless days of only work, she'd finally talked to him.

By that time, his wife had been gone for years, his daughters were away at school, and everyone in town either avoided him or started giving him advice on how he needed to live. Then, one day, she was standing by the west road tying a white tea towel on the fence.

He knew the signal for help and stopped.

They spent hours fighting together to get a tractor out of a ditch. They laughed at first at how hard the chore was, then they both yelled orders and cussed. When she tossed a dirt clod to get his attention, the fight was on. Two adults turned into children for a few minutes. Years seemed to melt away along with their worries.

As the day cooled, they ate sandwiches with mud caked on their faces. Then they lay in the grass to watch the sun go down in silence. His big hand took her small one. Neither said a word, but in that one moment both knew they'd never really let go.

He felt ageless that day and happy for the first time in years. Bear thought of that time as he drove toward her now.

No, he thought, *I feel like I am still alive. When I'm with her I'm all ages. I'm a kid watching a fairy run. I'm going off to the Army with a girl crying as she waves goodbye. I'm a man helping a woman and loving that she'd allow me to.* He took a deep breath and said, "A lifetime of short snapshots of living with her, loving her, of being hers."

The day he finally touched her, mud and all, the bond became clean. He thought back to that little girl with black hair flying around her as she ran, and then of the fairy waving him goodbye from the fence with tears running down her cheeks. He should have stopped and held her before he left home. Now, he realized, he'd loved her even then.

In the war when he was afraid, he swore he felt her freedom

and presence encouraging him to make it home. He promised when he finally got back, he'd tell her "thank you" for being with him.

But he hadn't.

And today, whether they'd have a few minutes alone or hours, he'd make another memory and store it away in his heart.

He'd been with a few women, but none like her. She rested easy in his heart and his thoughts.

Chapter 3

Andi's Storm

Monday

Andi Delane blew into the Honey Creek sheriff's office like a Texas tornado in full fury. Papers, posters, and a week's worth of mail flew around the bay of a room as if she planned to do spring cleaning. Everyone in the building turned to watch a woman obviously on a mission.

At five-feet-ten inches tall with brown eyes and sunshine hair tied in a bun, no one would miss her passing by. But at a second glance even the Hulk might take a step back. Andi Delane was a woman used to being in charge, and only a fool would get in her way.

A beefy deputy stood up from the information desk and bobbed his reddish-brown head in a greeting. "May I help you, ma'am?"

For a blink she wondered if they grew deputies oversized in this valley just to scare visitors. This guy looked just like the cop who gave her the ticket. He seemed to be playing with his computer.

Andi didn't have time for conversation with the town pumpkin, but she had to educate him. "Don't call me ma'am. Don't open doors for me and don't explain anything to me. Got it, Deputy?"

"Yes, ma'am." His eyes widened as if he realized he'd said something wrong, again. He looked directly at her now, but his big hand hovered over the keyboard.

"Where is the sheriff in this county?" she demanded as she moved toward the glass door to the only office visible.

The only other deputy in the room backed up, leaving a trail of coffee dripping from his full cup. Finally, he froze and pointed to the one office in the room.

Andi didn't bother to thank the mute deputy.

Without a sound, the sheriff stepped out of his office and straightened. He might be younger than she was, but he carried authority on his square shoulders and intelligence in his eyes. He gestured for her to follow him to his office.

In the room, she offered her hand. "Sheriff Pecos Smith, I assume. I'm Andi Delane, presently assigned to the Dallas Police Department as a detective. I was told to report to you and only you."

"I've been expecting you for months, Miss Delane. I wasn't sure of your last name. No one seemed to know where you were. I'm afraid I have some bad news to pass along." He shook her hand with a firm grip.

Andi almost smiled. "Thanks to your dogged hunt, I'm here. A friend, a Texas Ranger, convinced me to talk to you and my kin before you guys start nailing up 'missing person' posters across the country." She lowered her voice. "The ranger said you can be trusted. I often use other names when I'm on duty."

Pecos Smith nodded once. "Understood."

Andi felt like she knew this kid of a sheriff. As always, she'd done her research. Smith was a recent college grad. Father of two. Still in his twenties. Hero. A Texas Ranger she knew said Pecos Smith would be a legend before he was forty, if he lived. He was one of those rare people who ran toward danger when others needed help.

Lowering her voice she said, "Thanks for your time, Sheriff Smith."

"Of course. And it's Pecos to you. I've been hearing about you for so long, I feel like you're one of my long-lost cousins. May I offer you a coffee?"

"No. I won't take up much of your time."

She kicked the door closed behind them and took a seat when he pointed toward the one chair across from his desk. Andi removed her jacket as he picked up a pen. He'd obviously sensed the importance of what she was about to tell him.

Andi was thankful he didn't waste time with small talk as she slid both her driver's license and her Dallas PD badge toward him. "I'm also a pilot and don't wear a uniform."

The sheriff took a quick look at her IDs and passed them back across the desk. "How can I be of help? Should I call you Detective, Andi, or Miss Delane? I guess you already know your father passed away."

"The lawyer told my mother that he died. I never met him. And, as of now, you are my only friend in town." She took note that Pecos presented himself as calm, inquisitive, but listening to every word.

Andi continued, "I'll just tell folks I'm passing through. Taking time to see where I was born. I'll answer to Andi Delane if anyone asks, but I'd rather no one know any of my background at all, including your deputies."

The sheriff stared at her. "I'm aware there is another reason you're here, Andi." Pecos leaned closer. "Understand that this valley is not 'on the way' to anywhere, and the story that you are here to find long-lost relatives, though true, might raise some questions."

"That's valid, but I can handle it with no problem." She noted never to lie to Pecos. He read people too easily. Even her. "I'm due to testify on a drug trafficking case. My captain suggested I lay low for a few weeks, so I decided to visit kin I didn't even know I had until your town lawyer, Jackson Landry, informed me a man named me in his will."

Andi would not show any emotion over a bum who never claimed her or even saw her. Jamie Morrell was nothing more than a sperm donor in her life. "Mom called him once to tell him he had another child. But Jamie hung up on her before she told him I was a girl.

"My mother moved us to DC before I had time to remember this place. My real father is the man who raised me. Stood by my mother and still does. I want nothing from a man who didn't care if I was a girl or boy."

Pecos nodded. "I've heard those words about not wanting inheritance before. I've met two of your brothers." He hesitated then added, "Not many people know that Jamie Morrell's mother was a Delane. If you hate him, why'd you use that name?"

"It was convenient. I've used many others. Since I joined the department, I've worked undercover mostly. I was taught to use disposable names when I was working and I consider Delane disposable."

Pecos lifted a file. "I'm aware you served in the Army for six years as an MP before you signed on as an undercover cop with DPD. What I don't understand is why you've avoided coming here for over a year. Why show up now?"

She stared at him.

Pecos didn't blink.

Finally, she leaned close and said in a low voice, "Things got a little hot with my last undercover assignment. Until Dallas slows down, I thought I'd hang out here where no one will notice me. This place looks like the middle of nowhere. Good as anywhere. Even pretty in late fall, in fact, but I'll be gone before the first hard freeze."

Pecos leaned back. "No more questions, Andi. If I ask too many questions, I have a feeling that tall Texas Ranger will visit me again. Nice guy but he had a strange habit."

"What's that?"

"When the Ranger ordered me to stop looking for you if I wanted to stay walking, his left hand never left his Colt 1911."

"He threatened you!"

"No. I took it as if he was just asking about my health."

Andi couldn't help but smile. Ranger Carlson Ramm had been her mentor in the Army. He always had her back. He claimed his family had been Rangers for almost two hundred years. She thought back about the time she and Ramm spent together as soldiers. Once they could have been more, but it wasn't to be. It seemed she lived so much of her life in shadow, she wondered if there was an Andi to know in the real world at all anymore.

Straightening, her memories washed away and she focused on today.

Today was all that mattered. No past. No future. All she had was now. "While it's true I have no affection or care for Jamie Morrell, I would, however, like to know the names of the three men who Morrell also fathered. Because of the assignment I'm involved with, my family, no matter how distant, needs to be informed that they might be in danger. A year ago, I saw a criminal's face and he might try to get to me through them before he goes on trial—or even after."

She met his eyes. "All I just told you is between me and you."

Pecos nodded once. "You're just here to see the will and find out if you have any kin left in town. Right?" The sheriff smiled. "I've only met two of your half-brothers. If you'll tell me where you are staying in town, I'll arrange a meeting if they agree." He shook his head. "They'll be surprised you're a girl.

Jamie wrote his will the day he died and didn't know how to spell your name."

Andi lowered her voice. "It's critical that I locate my brothers now, Sheriff. I don't have any time to waste. Because of me, these men may be in danger."

Sheriff Smith studied her a moment and, without blinking, ordered, "Tell me all the facts you can about who might come after your brothers and I'll help, but, Andi, one of your half-brothers is just a boy."

"Find my brothers and I'll tell you all you need to know later."

The sheriff stood slowly as if trying to decide what to do. Finally, he answered, "I'll contact the two. But it will be up to them if and when they want to meet you."

Andi stood and stared at Pecos as if she planned to fight.

Smith didn't move. "Jackson asked me to find you and inform you that your father was dead, that's it. If you want my help, we do this my way or not at all. You may feel responsible for your brothers, but every man, woman, and child in this county is under my protection, and for all I know you're the one hunting them."

She didn't move as she took in one long breath and nodded. "I would do the same thing in your shoes." She offered her hand as a comrade this time, and they shook.

He opened his office door and she marched through. "It may take a while to round up your kin. You might want to walk around our town square while you wait. There's a café, a bakery, or good coffee in Noah's bookshop. A mile east of Main is a lodge circled with cabins. Good place to stay if you need a bed for the night with some privacy."

"How are you going to find me, Sheriff, if you locate them today?"

"I'll just look for a rental car. In a town this size it won't be hard."

"No car. Blue Jeep." She managed a quick smile. "I might

stay the night. I was born here, but once I'm finished I doubt I'll ever come back."

Andi walked out with only a nod. She didn't want to make an enemy, but she wasn't someone who made friends easily. Her logical mind said she might need the sheriff. All she'd been told was her father's name. She didn't even know her other siblings' last or first names. If the other women who got pregnant by Morrell never married him either, Andi wouldn't know where to start.

Her mother had married a soldier stationed in DC before Andi turned three. He was her father as far as Andi was concerned, but he never gave her his name, which bothered her some as she grew up. It was only when she went into the same branch of the Army that he had served in did Andi understand. He was protecting her by putting as much distance between his name and hers just in case someone tried to get to him through Andi or her mother. Leaving behind her MP badge for the Dallas Police Department turned out to be just as dangerous, as police departments were public entities with few secrets. It seemed danger had followed her all her life.

Now, three men she'd never met might be in trouble because of what she did for a living. Correction, two men and one child. And, thanks to the people in this little town, someone might figure out how she was connected to three half-brothers she'd never met.

When she walked by the beefy deputy at the front desk he stood. "Morning, again," he said with a goofy grin. "You be sure and come back if we can help you."

She decided she didn't have enough will left to straighten him out, and blood would probably flow onto Main Street, spoiling it, if she murdered him.

As she walked through the door, she glanced back. The sheriff was leaning on the doorframe of his office and the deputy nodded once toward Pecos.

Andi guessed the sheriff's silent command. She was about to have a tail.

The deputy stood and watched as she walked toward Main. The woman with eyes full of fire.

Now he could see all of her. Tall. Really tall. She wasn't stout, but slender like a long-distance runner. Long legs. Danny loved to watch long-legged women move. Graceful like a dancer in slow motion.

He grabbed his cover and headed out. If the sheriff wanted him to follow her, the deputy had no problem with the assignment.

She didn't look back. She was a woman on some kind of mission. He couldn't remember a female who interested him so completely. She was strong, fast talking, bossy, but those eyes still drew him. After college, when his heart healed from his first love, he'd meant to start dating again. Someone local. Someone he'd known forever.

But the memory of Karly always seemed too raw. The first time he kissed Karly Ann Clark, he thought she was his forever love, but it just wasn't meant to be. He figured at some point he'd start dating again, but as time passed, it was just easier to coast.

In the case of the woman he followed this afternoon, he didn't feel that she was date material. In fact, if she turned back and saw him, the only feeling he'd have was dread.

He frowned as he realized that she didn't even remember him. He was standing right by the driver's window giving her a ticket, and thirty minutes later in the sheriff's office she didn't see him. She only saw the uniform.

Danny imagined that Andi Delane had been one of those Amazon warriors who fought a thousand years ago. That type of imagery seemed to suit her. The way she looked, talked, and carried herself was regal, yet dangerous. Like the fanciest king cobra he'd ever seen, with sparkling eyes and hypnotic moves.

She stepped into the bookshop on Main and he slowed. With this assignment Danny thought that maybe he should pay the sheriff to come to work. How many jobs would list "follow a beautiful woman around town" as one of the duties? He could certainly live with that today. Beat sitting behind the lilac bushes on Highway 20 just to write traffic tickets. He sat down on a bench and watched her through the window.

She was so out of his league he wasn't sure he could carry on a conversation.

Maybe, if he followed her long enough, she'd ugly-up. Women tend to do that. Some have voices that irritate a man, or a habit that grates like fingernails on a chalkboard. Like putting a lock of hair in their mouth or always touching their jewelry as if he might grab it and run. And the worst, the girl who always adds *and* or *like* to the end of every sentence. That way she never has to pause when talking.

After a half hour, he saw no bad habit. In fact, she didn't even notice him. All his life Danny had always been the tallest or biggest one in the room except on the football field. But to her he seemed to be invisible, and at this moment, invisible was a new experience.

He was a perfect tail, he thought, as the trees around the square dropped the first leaves of fall in the breeze.

About the time he relaxed he saw a man take a seat at her tiny table and Danny's cop radar sprung to attention. It seemed a little too casual and almost innocent, but he could tell Andi was on high alert, and now so was he.

Chapter 4

Andi's Search

Monday

Andi was acting totally normal, or at least as normal as she imagined people acted in a small town with nothing to do. She'd left the sheriff's office at a brisk walk, but not too fast. She sat down inside the bookshop on the square and slowly drank the coffee that she'd been offered. Since the three other customers were sitting alone reading, Andi grabbed the first book she saw. The table she'd chosen allowed her to see both the store and the window. As always, she sat with her back to the wall.

Before she could open the book, a beanpole of a man with black-rimmed glasses appeared. "More coffee? I've got about a half a pot left and your refill is free."

Looking up she asked, "What kind of coffees you got?" This place might not be the coffee capital of Texas, but at least the owner knew how to talk. Northern, obviously. A bit of New York in his words.

"Just black. I've got packets of cream and sugar over by the counter; they're free." The man wasn't apologetic, just informative. "I usually also offer scones in the morning, but the Over the Hill walkers ate them all on the second loop around the square."

When she just stared at the bookshop owner, he added, "Since they increased to four laps, they feel they need something to keep going."

Andi almost rolled her eyes at him and wondered if all locals were as boring as cold scones. What made him think she cared about the town's senior citizens? "Just coffee, please. Black is fine."

"Coming right up."

As he walked away, Andi did what she always did. She took his measure. If someone asked her a month from now what he looked like, she'd remember all the stats right down to the tiny scar on his neck and his hair that didn't seem to be black or brown.

When he brought her coffee, he said, "Enjoy your cookbook."

The book in her lap was a cookbook? It's a wonder it didn't singe her hands, as the last place she'd be caught dead was a kitchen. She definitely needed caffeine. After a five-hour drive on a wild-goose chase she must have cracked up. She was much too detail oriented to not notice the book title. That attention to detail is what kept her alive undercover and she couldn't get sloppy now. She'd never read a cookbook or bought one, but she had to admit, the pictures on the front made her hungry.

It occurred to Andi that she might be losing her edge, but then she looked out the window and saw her tail, the deputy, sitting on a bench in plain sight. Okay, she had more of an edge than that and sincerely hoped someone remembered to tell him to come inside before it started to rain. Against her better judgment she had to acknowledge that the big guy was kind of cute. Not manly cute, but he had that goofy German shepherd puppy kind of cute, as if he had no clue how to be invisible and just enjoyed playing the game.

A short time later she was deep into the history of chuckwagon recipes when a shadow passed over her. Before she could look up, a man with a sidearm strapped to his leg sat down across from her as if he'd been invited. Both the chair and Andi groaned.

"Hello, Andi, mind if I join you?"

For a moment she had the urge to reach for her service weapon on her ankle, then he took his Stetson off. Longer hair, ten pounds heavier, same smile.

With a strong Texas accent, he said, "You lost, kid?"

No one had called her *kid* since she was a recruit at Lackland. He'd been a newbie captain, almost as green as she was. He was her trainer ten years ago and hadn't stopped bossing her around since.

"You are not my superior anymore, Major Ramm. You haven't been for years."

"Right. You know, Andi, that I changed from major to Texas Ranger. Thought the uniform was classier." Carl winked at her. Everyone knew the Texas Rangers didn't wear a uniform.

She smiled and Carl Ramm yelled his order for a cup of coffee. As soon as the bookshop owner delivered the cup, the once Army major started kidding her about how he hadn't known she was a girl for a week into training.

Andi didn't miss that he called the bookshop owner-waiter by name. Since Ramm was raised in El Paso, he had no reason to be in this tiny town in the middle of nowhere. She knew he was based out of Austin. Unless he was watching someone here, and that just might be her.

The sheriff mentioned him and now he shows up. Yep, the ranger was keeping tabs on her.

She leaned back and waited for him to stop the small talk.

The Texas Ranger knew something and she'd bet a hundred dollars that it was something he wanted her to know too.

When they started on their third cup, she got in a word. "What do you know, Major? You didn't drive over half the state to have coffee."

He took a deep breath and answered. "You know, Andi, you don't need to call me Major anymore. But you were always hard on turning anything loose."

"We've texted or talked a dozen times over the phone the past two years. I need to know you're doing well."

She turned toward the windows, her face blank of emotion but her mind echoing words from the past. *We're not friends, not lovers, not partners. Just keeping up.* Ramm drove over a hundred miles to check on her.

For a moment his face was hard, the face she'd seen when she'd walked away from him. He hadn't said one harsh word, but she knew whatever they had was gone.

His words came soft and low today. Almost a lover. Almost a friend. "We talk about work. Nothing else. That was your idea, kid."

Anyone listening would think they were friends simply catching up, but Andi saw a hundred words Carl wasn't saying. Feelings he couldn't identify. She was in Dallas and he was in Austin but neither made the three-hour drive. Somehow, he knew she'd taken a few days off and was here, where she was born.

"What do you know about my father, Ramm? That is the only reason I'm here in Honey Creek. But you already knew that."

"I don't know much. Just saw he died last year. I figured it would take a while for the news to reach you, but you'd come. I'm here to offer a shoulder to cry on or backup if you need it."

"Not your problem. I can handle it." She was not going to mention her brothers or the fact she'd be testifying in Dallas soon against a drug boss.

"I'll never forget we were once close friends, but that's over, I guess. You walked away without a word. That was cold, Andi."

"If I'd stayed one moment more we would have argued." She studied him. Ramm was a man who always thought he was right. Maybe he was most of the time, but he wasn't right for her.

He showed no emotion but his whole body stiffened. "Today, I'm just here as a ranger, seeing if you need any help." He slid a folder across the table. "Found little about the person on your birth certificate. He was a trucker with no close friends. Every place he lived in the valley was a rental. Always listed his occupation as trucker. Never lived in a place longer than a year."

She studied the papers. "You wouldn't be here unless you thought I needed you." She stared directly at him. "And while I'm at it, Ranger, stop keeping up with me. We're not in the service anymore, and I'm officially on vacation. I'm no longer your problem."

His hard eyes never stopped staring. "You'll always be my problem. It's like a piece of you is buried inside me."

"It's over," she said softly. She didn't want to hurt him, but he had a trait she couldn't live with. Ranger Carlson Ramm always had to be the lead, the boss, the best. Everything had to be his way or the highway, so finally she took the highway and left. The talent that made him a leader flawed him as a lover.

Neither said another word. They both had a past that needed to remain buried.

She stood and dropped a five on the table and walked away. If she looked back at him, even for a moment, she'd remember too much.

His order followed her. "Call me if you need me."

"I will," she lied.

A flock of gray-headed ladies in jogging suits, all rainbow colors, rushed in. They said hello as if they knew her and began gathering their things behind the counters. Apparently, the bookshop was their locker and the owner had to jump out of their way.

Without looking back at Ramm, Andi moved to the door. Maybe she'd walk the town square. As always Andi felt there wasn't air around when the major was close.

Finally, the last few straggling Over the Hill joggers made it into the bookshop to collect their things. Andi held the door and nodded goodbye to every one of them for no reason at all.

Then she scanned the store.

Ranger Carl Ramm was gone. Probably lost in the stacks. He usually had a book with him, half a dozen in his car. He might live in the real world at work, but off duty he lived in Western novels. Maybe he got to know Noah O'Brien by dropping by his shop, nothing else.

She closed her eyes and screamed inside her head. "You're not mine and I'm not yours. I never will be." She needed to let go of him and he needed to let go of her.

When she finally opened her eyes, the bookshop owner was staring at her. "You all right?"

"No. Something is broken."

The guy smiled and said, "We've got a repair shop next door. Bear Buchanan can fix anything."

She stepped into the sun and walked to her rented Jeep knowing what was broken could not be fixed. It wasn't the Jeep; it was her heart.

Danny watched her climb into her vehicle, drive to the other side of the square and park in front of the café. He took a bench in the center of the town square. The old elms swayed in the breeze as if they were brushing him out of view of people. Out of view of Andi Delane.

She didn't get out. It was too late for breakfast and too early for lunch. She just sat there staring out the windshield. She was killing time, which told Danny a great deal. No friends in town to drop in on and she wasn't in Honey Creek to shop. She wasn't hungry or she would go in and order in the empty café.

She had nowhere to go and no friends to talk to. Andi Delane was a loner. She wasn't just a lone wolf, and from what he could see, she liked it that way.

Another fact he mentally noted was that she was comfortable in her skin. She was looking for something, and Danny had a feeling the woman with fiery eyes wouldn't be leaving until she found it.

"Let me help you," he said under his breath. His fiery-eyed lady was in some kind of trouble, he could feel it. It clung to her like a silky spiderweb you walk through and can't leave behind. Hell, as far as he knew she might always be in danger. He could almost taste it in the air. Danger might blow around her like a spring storm, but he wasn't going anywhere.

He almost said the words aloud. *I'm not going anywhere, lady. Danger or not, I've got your six.*

Chapter 5

Catching an Angel

Monday

Bear Buchanan didn't bother to check the little farmhouse when he climbed out of his truck. Eliza wouldn't be inside before dusk anyway. In long, sure strides, he stormed into the barn. "Eliza! Where are you?" he yelled.

Silence, except for the horses in their stalls and one lost chicken that had wandered into the barn.

Bear took two more strides forward and stood in the middle of Eliza's barn and yelled, "I've told you a dozen times that old refrigerator needs to be replaced. I swear you don't listen. I brought another one just in case I can't fix the old box."

He heard movement in the loft. "Eliza! I don't have all day to play games. Are you up in the loft or am I talking to this dumb chicken?" With his fists on his belt and his legs wide, Bear Buchanan felt like he was ready to fight, except for the slight smile raising the corner of his lips.

When she appeared, she was laughing. "Catch me, Bear." She jumped from the barn loft as if she was free as a bird. For a moment his fairy was flying.

Bear let out a few cusswords as Eliza dropped into his arms. He held her tight for a while as if he couldn't let her go. "Don't do that, honey. Every time you stop my heart. You're in your late forties and I'm partway to sixty. I should never have ordered you to kiss me that day. Since then, you think I'm your toy."

"You didn't tell me to kiss you. I ordered you to kiss me. I'm younger, so my memory is better. I just couldn't wait any longer to be close." She wiggled out of his arms and climbed up a rung of the loft ladder.

He was almost eye to eye with her now. He smiled and said, "No, I told you to kiss me and you did. And I think that was the last time you listened to me." He pressed her against the ladder. "I do love kissing you, but I like arguing with you even more. You get mad and start beating on me and I start lightly touching you. I win every fight."

"Not every time." She hurried out of his grip.

He brushed his fingers through her black hair, now peppered with white, as she moved up the ladder, but made no effort to slow her flight.

"Hurry up, old man, or I'll start without you."

When he stepped onto the barn's loft floor, she squealed and disappeared behind a stack of hay.

As always, he knew where she was headed. Once he found her, he took a moment to stand over her beautiful form resting in a blanket on their hay bed. His mind needed a moment to snap a memory to keep forever. She was petite and tanned from the sun. Her curls hung free to her waist. Lowering next to her, neither said a word. The bear was gentle and the lamb was demanding. They laughed and loved as longtime lovers do.

Shadows spread and the afternoon passed while Bear folded his arms around her and murmured that he loved her. She placed her hand over his heart as they drifted to sleep.

As twilight shaded the loft, she laced her fingers in his and said, "If I die, I'll come back a moment before night falls and lay my hand over yours so you'll know I'm still with you."

"And if I die first?"

She was silent for a while, then she answered, "You are the strongest man I've ever seen. If you are heaven-bound, reach back to earth and pull me up with you. I don't want to be here without you."

Kissing her forehead he told her, "I'm the luckiest man in the world."

He kissed her until she pushed him away. "You have to go. I hear the evening train."

"You know, Eliza, marry me and we could sleep every night together. I know you won't leave your land, but I'd like to live with you and when we get restless, I'll show you places all over the world."

"Someday," she said.

She cuddled against him as she asked, "What about your girls?"

Bear sat up. "They're big enough to turn out to graze." That made her laugh, but he didn't smile. He knew there would be hell to pay if his daughters ever knew about them. His oldest, Katherine, might not know Eliza enough to care about her, but she cared about herself and his money enough to circle the wagons if she thought he might marry someone. Cora, his youngest, would just be hurt he'd kept it from her, and he couldn't bear to hurt her.

Eliza was silent for a while. Finally, she said, "I love us just the way we are. Stay with me until dawn. Stay so late that your warmth comforts me even hours after you've left. I belong next to you."

". . . and I you." As always, he pulled her closer. Their longing for one other when they were apart was woven into the material of their love, somehow making it more precious.

She patted his chest. "Want to stay for a late supper?"

"What are you having?"

"Everything that's thawed."

She described every rattle and cough the fridge made as she stood in front of Bear and he dressed her. Over the years he'd discovered he loved dressing her almost as much as undressing her.

Love overflowed inside him. He wasn't hungry, but he'd take every minute of time he could steal with his precious fairy.

Chapter 6

Watching Bear's Bull Run

Noah O'Brien was so bored on Wednesday he decided to sweep the bookshop. Since he'd opened at nine, people had wandered in one at a time. Most of them just wanted coffee and to complain about the weather. The cloudy October day made it seem late in the afternoon.

Noah tried to look busy so he didn't have to talk about the weather on repeat the rest of the day.

The coffee was almost gone when Cora Lee Buchanan rushed in. Noah didn't have to look at a clock. He knew it was her lunch hour.

Cora Lee was Bear's youngest and seemed more just out of high school than late into her twenties. She was quiet, a first-grade teacher, and shy. In three years, he couldn't remember her looking directly at him. She also lived on the second floor, two apartments down, but he never heard music or a TV. She was one of the few people he could say mirrored his own quietness, and that was a great quality in a neighbor. No one had ever rented the place between them. Now and then he thought that they were living together upstairs and no one noticed, not even them.

On Wednesday when Bear's offspring came in, Noah usually listened to the oldest of Bear's daughters, Katherine, complain about her life or at least one of her ex-husbands. No matter how she started her woes, she ended with her father's shortcomings. He worked too much. He never gave her enough money to make her dreams come true. Her father's shop smelled like oil, paint, and dust. After giving up on him cleaning the place years ago, Katherine simply refused to go into Bear's Fix-It Shop.

So, Noah had to suffer her company every Wednesday. The only blessing to soften the blow was he got to see Cora Lee as well. She was reserved and patient; now and then she'd laugh at something her big sister said. Like when Katherine argued that if there was a ghost in the bookshop, he'd be watching Katherine because not even a spirit would notice Noah or Cora.

Kat would always whine that Bear must have figured out fast that the girls picked him up for lunch every first Wednesday to ask for something. Katherine usually hugged her father, air kissed his cheek, then began with, "We've got a great deal to talk about, Father. After all, it is Wednesday."

When Bear finally did come in to take them to lunch, he never listened to Katherine complain, and Noah had noticed Bear hugged his youngest longer. She was closer to his heart.

Katherine was between husbands and seemed to come home to whine. Which, according to gossip, meant she was milking her dad for money to buy a condo in Aspen. She claimed she'd put the place in Bear's name and would live there only until she remarried.

"I don't want a ski lodge to keep up with when I do find my rich skier," she exclaimed last month. "I hate snow, but for some reason unmarried men buy in Aspen." Then she'd smiled that smile she'd perfected when she was Homecoming Queen. "It won't cost you anything, Father. You can sell it and make enough to pay for my next wedding."

Bear always offered the empty apartment upstairs, and

Katherine would turn it down saying something about only moles would live up there. Then silently all the Buchanans would stand and walk across the street to the café. The girls never looked hungry, and Bear always looked trapped.

The only problem with this routine was Bear seemed to forget it was Wednesday, and his memory loss now became Noah's problem. Katherine was like a scratched record that kept playing her father's shortcomings while the girls waited next door at the bookshop for Bear to come out of, in Kat's words, the smelly, greasy, dusty repair shop. Noah watched every Wednesday's dance but was always glad when it was over.

Usually, once Bear checked his phone, locked up, and taped a faded sign to the door that said simply GONE, then he'd walk into Noah's place and act like he was surprised to see his daughters.

Today, as always, Katherine did all the talking until Cora wandered off to examine the new children's books Noah ordered every month for her. With her sister gone, Katherine turned her frustration toward Noah. "Mr. O'Brien, are you telling me you don't have any idea where my father is?"

"Not a clue, Miss Buchanan." Noah tried to look busy.

"You do know it is Wednesday, Mr. O'Brien?"

"I do."

"Did you mention that to my father? How hard could it be to yell at him when he walks by your door? Just say, *Morning, Bear. Nice Wednesday.*"

"Can't do that."

Kat looked like she might cuss. "Why not?"

He glanced at the windows. "It's rainy and cloudy today." Doing his best to sound uninterested rather than sarcastic.

She rolled her eyes as if she'd just noticed she'd been talking to a rabbit.

Noah had had enough. "Sorry, Miss Buchanan, but I didn't

see Bear-tracking in the lease when I signed on to rent this place." He fought down a laugh. "But I'll check the terms."

He held a random flyer close to his face as if it was the lease document and pretended to read, "Let me see: Open every day but Sunday. Pay on the first. Keep up with Bear. Remind said Bear what day it is every Wednesday."

She gave him a look that could only mean *Go to hell.*

When Noah glanced over at Cora Lee, the younger sister silently lowered her head out of sight as if she'd already heard mortars flying in. He would swear he'd seen the flash of a grin though.

He poured the last of the coffee in a cup and walked around the counter. He calmly sauntered to the children's section of the store. Cora Lee didn't look up but she handed him three books and took the coffee.

"I wish I could help, but I don't know where your father is. Bear doesn't report to me, and I get the idea he wouldn't thank me for taking on the job."

The greenest eyes he'd ever seen finally looked at him. "I understand, Mr. O'Brien. My pop marches to his own beat."

Katherine's voice butted in loud enough to wake the ghosts on the third floor. "My name is not Buchanan, Mr. O'Brien. I gave away that name for greener pastures and a few others about ten years ago. I don't believe in looking back in life. I'm about to start dating David Henry Weatherly, so I probably will be Mrs. Weatherly, if my father will take the time to talk to me. I want to be settled in Aspen by spring and married by fall, so I won't have to deal with snow." She had to brag. That Homecoming Queen smile came out. "Of course, David has four homes. Once we marry, we will travel each season, living in New York in spring. Quebec in summer. Europe in fall. Florida in winter. I plan to make him understand that we'll have no need for Aspen."

Noah couldn't care less where Bear Buchanan was, but he

44 / Jodi Thomas

clearly understood why he wasn't here. Katherine was still talking but Noah gave up on listening. He'd learned three weeks ago that if he did butt in on Katherine's rattling, she'd just rewind and say the same thing all over again.

Cora Lee brought her half-empty cup back and told her sister that she had to get back to school. She patted the three picture books on the counter. "I'll pick these up before you close."

Noah nodded toward Katherine and murmured to Cora Lee, "Aren't you forgetting something?"

Cora Lee's green eyes met his for the second time today.

She let out a tiny laugh only Noah could hear. "I can't take her to school. Not allowed. Last time she visited my class, she told the kids that being the school queen made her royalty, and that was more important than the principal."

"Well, everyone knows that's true." He winked at Cora Lee. She turned away but she was smiling.

Three older women wearing floppy rain hats and rain-slickers rushed in as if Noah was having a sale.

"My, oh, my," the first one said, "I can't believe it's Katherine Buchanan back in town. Honey, you look better every time I see you. I can't understand why one of the men in town didn't snap you up before you went to college. One semester and you had a ring."

Another lady noticed Cora. "Morning, Miss Buchanan. My granddaughter loves your class."

Before Cora could answer, the dripping lady turned back to Katherine.

Noah watched Cora Lee drop a dollar in the coffee jar and slip out unseen by the ladies fawning over Katherine's dress.

The Homecoming Queen hugged the ladies as she explained she was just in town to check on her father. "I'm staying with my aunt in Waco while I'm relocating. I just have to come home now and then to make sure he hasn't had a stroke or something. He's getting older, you know." Katherine looked so sad Noah wondered if Atlanta was burning again. Maybe the next dress would resemble drapes.

Noah doubted Katherine remembered any of the ladies' names, but she told them all about the wonderful condo she was buying in Aspen.

At a break in the chatter Noah added a fact. "She doesn't go by Buchanan. Bear told me last week that his oldest daughter might end up with more last names than our phone book."

Two of the ladies before him laughed. Katherine walked right past the coffee jar and out the door. When the ladies were told there was no more coffee, they left for the café.

Noah just stood watching the women and enjoying the silence of his shop. In the calm, he remembered something. He'd heard Cora Lee's shy, light laughter somewhere before.

Two nights ago. On the roof. He'd heard her. Though he never saw her in the pitch black, he knew she was there.

Chapter 7

Bear's Break

Friday

Bear Buchanan went into his shop an hour earlier than usual. The lights weren't even on at the bookshop but Bear had work to do. Funny thing about broken washers or toasters, or even printers, customers seemed to think that no matter what day they brought them in all shattered, he should have the machine fixed by closing time on Friday.

When he turned the light on, he always smiled. His projects were lined up waiting to be reborn.

First up today was Nancy Tyler's old mixer whose beaters wouldn't beat together. The mixer was yellow, telling Bear that Nancy had had the thing thirty years or more. Bear would clean the motor up and put new beaters in, then charge her five dollars.

Next on the operating table was old man Adams's lawn mower. He mowed his grass year-round, and in the summer heat mowed well after dark with only a headlamp for light. Because of that, he decapitated at least one sprinkler head a month. Bear thought about charging Adams double. Half for replacing at least one blade and half for having to listen to Adams complain about his wife.

Mrs. Adams only came in once. Sweet lady. She asked if he fixed hearing aids. When he said no, she giggled and turned around. He watched her walk to the old Ford her husband was sitting in. All the way she was shaking her head and smiling.

Bear worked through lunch but stopped long enough to pick up a few books from Noah. Then, like every Friday, he locked up at four and disappeared. Everyone knew he turned off his phone once he left town. Bear let everyone assume that he farmed on weekends, or rested, or read.

In fact, Bear didn't care what folks thought he did. Whenever his daughters left for school or traveled with aunts every summer, he was a ghost on weekends.

People gave up asking questions. After all, they'd reasoned, if it was interesting, he would have talked about it.

As he headed out of town, toward not his place but Eliza's Holly Rim, he grinned. The clouds might promise rain, but he didn't care; it was Friday, his favorite day.

A few hours later Eliza laughed when he relayed the secret to the Adams couple's perfect marriage. She never heard a harsh word from him thanks to her broken hearing aids.

Bear opened the loft doors so they could see the autumn sunset. He loved lying on their blanket in the loft. As the sun dropped slowly, so did the temperature. He knew she'd cuddle in beside him. He might be a foot taller, but somehow they fit together. He generally liked folks for the most part, but she went to town only when she had to. They'd never had a date. No dinners out. No movies. No county fairs. No town meetings. No weekends in a big city.

Neither cared. They had each other.

"I love you," he whispered as he kissed her head.

"I know."

Bear pulled her closer. She was already his, just like he was hers. He sometimes wished they would be together all the time, but, like a wild animal, she resisted being tamed. She couldn't be forced into a life she didn't want and he couldn't leave his herd. He rolled on his side so he could see her face. "Tell me one of your family's stories."

Once, she told him her great-grandfather, a full-blood Apache, wrote down on paper all the legends and myths about her land. *The Secrets of Holly Rim*, he named the little book. He wrote down things like how they farmed in the moon's light and how he slept on the rim the night he took a wife so he could show all the stars what a lucky man he was.

Bear didn't care much about the stories; he just loved her whispering in his ear as lovers did.

Her grandfather inherited the handwritten book and made copies for the next generation.

But years later one of the traveling preachers declared it "the devil's work," so his little books of stories about the rim were destroyed.

In the darkness of night, Eliza told a few of the tales as if they were great secrets passed down in the silence of midnight. Bear wished she remembered more. Like where the tribe disappeared at the turn of the century, but the few elders who remembered took the secret with them, and Eliza had been a little girl when the stories were passed to her.

Gently he picked his precious love up and carried her as he left the loft. Once he reached the ground, she cuddled into his arms and rested her head on his chest. There was no need to talk; they both knew what was about to happen. They'd eat dinner by a low fireplace in her log home, then she'd read what she'd written in her newest children's book. Her stories were not dark like the Apache legends. Her tales were poems about nature or gentle myths about talking animals for children she'd never meet.

Bear always smiled when Cora Lee bought one of Eliza's books. His teacher-daughter was reading her first-graders the stories written by his forever-lover.

Every Friday when Bear and Eliza were alone, they'd talk about everything and nothing. She knew about nature, and history, and the stars. Bear said little, but her stories calmed his soul. When he was with her, all the world was right.

Rain tapped on the metal roof as he mentally walked through their life together. No one knew how much she meant to him. The little girl who, in his mind, had followed him to war. The woman who came to him without a word. A lover, a friend, the only one who would ever hold his heart, all wrapped up in Eliza.

When the fire died, she'd take him by the hand and pull him toward her bed. Like everything surrounding Eliza there were no games or teasing, just a gentle coupling.

Friday night was heaven and he lived for that one night. One night. Twice would have been too much in a week. Less would be starvation. Once in a while, when the desire built to a burning need, they shared the dawn together.

He'd usually slip away before she woke. She'd remain in his thoughts, but he couldn't return. The rules had been set the first night years ago.

All Saturday and Sunday Bear worked his farm. He had to be exhausted so he wouldn't be tempted to return to paradise.

He asked her to marry him every time he touched her. His way of telling her that she was his world.

Chapter 8

Andi's Tail

Friday

Andi Delane worked with her computer propped on the tiny desk in the back cabin hidden among the trees. The sheriff had given her a good tip about the place. Silent. Private. Clean. She'd rented it so she could be close to town. Digger, the owner of the rustic cabins, told her the town woke at dawn.

Because of all the trees, the sun seemed to be sleeping later. She liked exploring nature, maybe because Andi had always thought she was wilder than most people. Every wild place had its soul. Each had its own personality. Her pop used to say that if you sleep somewhere for a week, a place seeps into your essence and you'll never forget it. The smell, the sounds, the feel of the air.

Unfortunately, the whole cabin smelled of the burned beans someone had tried to cook for supper a few nights ago, and every shutter rattled when the wind blew.

To make her headache worse, the email from headquarters said it was still too hot to come back home. They feared, because she would be testifying, a drug cartel had a bounty out on her. Besides there were too many questions floating in her mind about Honey Creek. Meeting at least two of her brothers. Reading Morrell's will.

Andi might be stuck in this town for a week with nothing to do but dig into a past she knew zero about. They would notify her when she needed to ID the perp in court. This quiet place was as good as any.

She turned off her laptop and put on her running shoes. When she slipped out the back window, she stood still to let her eyes adjust. The deputy was leaning against a tree five feet off the porch. He hadn't heard her, which was good.

It rolled around in her mind that the sheriff couldn't seem to find her half-brothers. He said something about her older brother telling his boss he was going on a hunting trip. That was the bad news. She'd have to wait to warn brothers she didn't even know that they might be in danger.

With a possible extended stay, she was even more grateful that Pecos had told her about this old cluster of fishing cabins at the edge of town. She could come and go without anyone seeing her, including the deputy. Hotels always had too many people around. These cabins were scattered between hundred-year-old trees with branches that touched the ground. The creek ran on one side and the back of the place was wild land, too rocky and uneven to have trails.

The sheriff said her half-brothers would probably be back in a few days, a week at the most. It was much longer than she intended to hang around, and with this town being so small, people would start to get friendly. It was inconvenient to be noticed too much.

Andi decided she'd have to blend in more. After dawn she'd buy a few pairs of jeans and three Clifton College sweatshirts to appear as more of a local. She was good at fitting into new places, but that would be hard here with a tail—especially an obvious mountain of a tail.

She thought of pistol-whipping him and letting him sleep it

off in the woods, but his head was probably as hard as a rock and the bounce back alone might break her wrist.

It wouldn't be horrible if he wasn't so obvious. It was like having a big Texas longhorn following you around and thinking he is invisible. If this was going to go on for a week there was no way people in town wouldn't notice and talk. That would blow everything. She'd heard him circling the cabin as if she wouldn't hear the world's biggest raccoon. He'd even sat outside the café, eating a candy bar, when she ate dinner earlier.

The only time she didn't see him was when she slipped in the sheriff's station's back door to see if Pecos had heard from her half-brothers. When she returned, there was her deputy dog acting like he was holding up the back wall of the sheriff's office.

The last couple nights she'd hear him moving outside around her cabin for a while like Bigfoot, then silence. She thought then that maybe her tail went home to take a bath and eat a meal. She hoped. The guy was growing on her with his constant "Morning, ma'am."

The deputy was always back at dawn.

The folks in town smiled at Deputy Obvious but didn't talk to her. After all, she was a stranger. She couldn't ask if anyone remembered her mother, and she had no idea what her brothers' names were. She also couldn't mention Jamie Morrell. That would blow her cover and have everyone asking questions. In short, she had no leads and few ideas. Small towns are the toughest places to get information on the down-low. Too many people in everyone's business.

As far as anyone here knew she was just on vacation. If the Texas Ranger she once served with hadn't told the sheriff about her, Pecos wouldn't have been waiting for her. And if she hadn't tried to order Pecos around, maybe the sheriff wouldn't have put a tail on her. But here she was.

The man who raised her was high enough in the government

to stop any inquiries into Andi's background. And her mother wouldn't say anything about the guy who'd "knocked her up" when she was eighteen. The only reason Andi knew the sperm donor's name and hometown at all was because of her birth certificate. Jamie Morrell was nothing more than a shadow in her life and she would like it to stay that way.

Pop, her stepdad, was her father. Every weekend she used to claim she was in bootcamp. They mountain climbed before she was ten, deep dived the next summer, flew before she drove a car. Pop never said he wished for a boy; he wanted Andi, his girl, who could take care of herself. He'd taught her to survive.

But once last year she broke a rule when she was undercover. She used her nickname, Andi. Andilana was her real name, but her mother had always called her Andi.

Andi wanted to use her name. She thought it was common enough no one would notice. They were going on a small bust. Only her team would call her Andi.

The raid went as planned, except for the fact that one of the perps heard her name and now she had to stay off the radar and far away from Dallas until things calmed down.

Hopefully soon, she'd testify against the suspect, ID him in court, and go back to her ghost life with dyed hair and another name. She'd only be in this little valley for a few weeks at the most. No one would think to look for her here. This place would vanish from her memory.

Once she was sure the deputy was gone for the fourth night, Andi slipped out of her cabin to a midnight sky and stretched. For a few moments someone might have heard her blending with the night, then only silence. When she was far away, she began running over wild, uncharted hills without making a sound. She always felt free in unbroken land. Deep down she knew she'd never settle down, get married, or stay in one place long enough to let the seasons all change. A part of her would always be a loner.

Since she knew the deputy had left, Andi thought she'd run for an hour, then maybe get some sleep.

The moon was high when she returned to the cabin. She stripped in the glow of her window's low light, then ran to the creek and waded silently into the cold water.

Thirty minutes later after a brisk swim she ran back to her window. No one had seen her. At this moment she was totally alone. Wild. Silent. Solitary.

She stood, still dripping, as the cool night breeze blew her hair dry and the moon's light made her skin glow.

One minute later she climbed in bed nude and closed her eyes. No one in Dallas knew anything about this town. "No one is chasing me," she kept telling herself. She knew it was most likely true, but a small bud of anxiety she couldn't place reared its ugly head. It had only happened a few times over the years, and she knew that sixth sense had saved her more than once. She'd slipped from one alias to another when she went undercover and then stepped into a nothing town barely on a map, so logic deemed the feeling to have no credence.

She was overplaying the problem. Seeing monsters where there were none. Making assumptions not based on fact.

If the Texas Ranger hadn't shown up to talk to the sheriff, she wouldn't be worried. He probably went back to Austin after getting her all confused. They weren't friends anymore. They didn't work together, and the affection they once had was ashes, but he still kept up. While he was the best at finding people, the idea that if he could find her, someone else could too, stuck with her.

A noise came from out back of the cabin. She glanced at the time. About the hour her beefy raccoon normally returned. Deputy Davis was probably digging through her trash right now, and that was actually a relief tonight.

She sat up and watched the side window. A porch light over

the cabins' office, fifty feet away, allowed just enough light to see anything moving in the shadows.

"Wait for it," she said under her breath. "Wait for it."

Snap. Snap and suddenly a howl came like a wounded coyote. She giggled behind her hand covering her mouth.

She wanted to yell for the deputy to stop digging in her trash, but half a dozen mouse traps loaded and ready would teach him a lesson.

"Go away, Deputy!"

"I'm just doing my job!" he yelled back.

"Great," she said. He was right. The guy was just doing his job and she was being intentionally spiteful. It bothered her a little but eventually she drifted off to sleep.

The next morning, he was sitting in his truck halfway between the cabin and the bookshop. The deputy looked terrible. He'd been sleeping under a tree for two nights, then he'd sat outside all day and was living on candy bars.

He was just doing his job echoed through her mind.

When she walked into the bookshop, Noah poured her a coffee without being asked. "In early this morning, lady with no name. You want a scone today?"

"No, thanks." She should have talked to the owner of the bookshop more. He was nice. Probably not an assassin or a drug dealer, but she'd assumed she would only be here a short time. Now it was awkward.

Noah moved away. Maybe he'd run out of conversation.

Andi straightened. "May I ask a favor, Noah?"

He turned toward her, seemingly surprised she could talk. "If I can."

She pointed to the deputy sitting outside. "Would you take a couple of scones and the biggest coffee you got to the deputy out there?"

He stared at her for a few seconds and then nodded.

He was already bagging the pastry when she said, "I'll pay. You do see him, right?"

"Of course. The whole town has watched Danny follow you around. We know he's tailing you, probably because the sheriff told him to. We all think he's doing a good job. It's not easy to be invisible when he's pushing 280 pounds. Folks say when he played football for Texas Tech no one could get past him. Said he could have gone pro, but he got injured."

Noah put the lid on the coffee and picked up the bag of scones. "I'll be back, so keep an eye on the shop, please."

She stood and put her hand over his that held the bag. "I need to do this myself."

Understanding eyes looked over his glasses. "Probably a good idea."

She knew he got it.

As she walked toward the bench the deputy was sitting on, she noticed his clothes were wrinkled and dirty in places. He didn't look at her and she thought he was sleeping with his eyes open.

She held out the coffee. "I've come to say I'm sorry." She saw two knuckles still had red scabs. "It's just I don't like being watched."

He didn't look angry. "I was just contemplating my life choices. I have no idea why I got this assignment." He glanced at her and took the coffee and scones. "I'm not stalking you. I like to think I'm just watching over you, that's it. I sure would feel bad if you got hurt on my watch, though the mousetraps last night tempted me to rethink that. We got two men out with the flu, so I'm working round the clock."

She smiled at him for the first time. "Look, Deputy, I'm only going to be here for a few days. How about I try to make it easy on you? I'll let you know when I'm moving from one place to another. Since everyone knows you're"—she hesitated, then continued—"watching over me, why don't we eat meals together? If you're sitting across the booth from me at the café, you'll be warm and get a real meal, and I think the sheriff would agree you're doing a great job."

He smiled and she thought he looked five years younger.

She leaned a little closer. "We'll have to set a few rules, though."

He frowned. "If the rules do not interfere with my job, or include mousetraps, I'm in."

"Agreed."

When he smiled, she saw the kindness. Now she felt really bad about last night. He was being very kind about the whole mess and the least she could do was be civil. Besides, if she was getting along with everyone's favorite deputy in town, then maybe she could get some of the information she needed without any nosy busybodies being the wiser.

While the deputy ate his second scone, she quickly shared the rules she'd made up on the spot. "I'm not doing anything illegal so I don't have to tell you anything. I will not hide from you, but don't follow too close. You cannot follow me into the restroom and do not take a picture of me."

He nodded and added, "You might follow a few rules, too, like don't stand in an open window when you get back from a swim." The corner of his lips lifted in a half smile. "Unless you just want to."

Andi rolled her eyes. "Forget what you saw, Deputy."

"Not a chance."

Andi had never been shy. "Then enjoy yourself and I'll blacken those eyes if you ever mention it to anyone."

"You are beautiful," the deputy said, "but I guess you know that, so it puts a lot of questions in my mind as to what you are doing spending time in Honey Creek."

"I will not answer any questions, Deputy. Don't try to interrogate me."

"I won't. I don't even know how. I'm not sure I remember

how to talk to any female, let alone a spicy, feisty one. I'm just doing my job watching over you." He met her eyes. "We don't have to chat or be friends, but understand that if you need help, I'm close."

A shiver slid down Andi's spine. She knew he was serious but wasn't sure if that was a good thing or a bad thing. She focused on her plan. She'd find out all she needed to know about the people in this town through him, and he wouldn't even know he was helping her get the information she needed.

As they sat on the bench while he drank his coffee, she felt a bit guilty. She was used to dealing with smugglers, cheaters, and killers. The deputy was clearly a good guy, and she hadn't run into many of them in her life.

He suddenly snorted. "If you start feeding me, folks will think you're my girl."

Andi hesitated a minute as the idea turned over in her mind. "Would that be so bad?" She realized the deputy had a great idea. Maybe people would talk to her more if she was linked romantically with a local. She wouldn't have to go through the sheriff or press Ranger Carlson Ramm for information. Maybe all she needed to do was stand next to Deputy Davis, bring him cookies or something and the townsfolk would be more friendly.

When she glanced back at him, he smiled. "I don't mind at all."

Andi closed her eyes and considered her plan. The things she didn't think twice about doing to criminals, you just didn't do to regular people. She'd gone from professional cop to selfish user overnight. She'd spent most of her life running into places where the bad guys lived. She routinely lied to everyone around her, knowing she'd be shot if anyone saw a crack in her cover. Now and then she had to fight her way out, destroying everything around her, and right this moment she was worrying about breaking this big guy's heart. It shouldn't be a big deal, but for some reason it just seemed wrong.

She was the best in her field—tough, skilled with all weapons—but after ten years she was drained. After she'd fought and ran and lied to do her job, she rested for a moment in between assignments and dreamed of a calmer world. A world where there was time for smiles, love, and trust. There had to be a place where she could sleep without being on alert or afraid, with people who would protect her as much as she protected herself.

The Lion of Lucerne flashed in her mind. A lion carved on a wall of rock in Switzerland. The brave lion is dying, as he lies on his shield. A monument to Swiss guards who died in the French Revolution in 1792. They were all from a little town in Lucerne. A generation of men lost.

Andi feared someday she'd die atop her shield without ever really living. Sometimes she felt she had trained her whole life to be a good soldier, to fight for right, but she was never taught to live.

Danny Davis watched as Andi walked back to the bookstore. There was something heavy about the way her shoulders hung, a burden she carried that pricked his curiosity. The vision of her in the moonlight had played through his mind on repeat since last night, and that was what he was thinking about when she brought over the scones, not that he would have told her that. She was attractive, for sure, but more than that, she was interesting.

As she settled in at a table in the bookstore, he thought back to that day eight years ago. It still played like a vivid horror story in his mind, just as it had every time he allowed his memories to surface. The worst day of his life was like a picture album covered in mud. The last day in college. The parties. His girl, who wore his engagement ring, laughing as they talked of the future.

They'd just graduated that morning when Danny walked into his best friend's dorm room. Two graduation gowns had been thrown on the floor along with a suit and a dress. His friend was nude on top of Danny's equally naked fiancée. They were both moaning and groping each other until they saw Danny.

The world stopped for a second. Love died. He could have sworn he heard his heart crack and even now could feel that jolt of pain and suffering in the moment.

"The day it stops hurting, I'll take Karly's picture down off the closet frame," he whispered to himself.

That memory made him swear off all the fairer sex all the years since.

He'd had his future planned with her. Graduate. Get married. Go pro for a few years. By thirty he'd have enough money, thanks to football, and then he'd quit and buy land. All his life he'd been too big. Too big for the chair in school. *We don't carry your size. Watch the door. Don't break anything. How is the air up there?*

Danny had always wanted his own place made to fit him. A place where he didn't have to duck through the doorway when he entered a room.

But all his dreams died that one day, that one moment. The shock of seeing them, the shouting, the fight, and then the accident. His best friend ran after him. They fought on the stairs. Both tumbled down the concrete steps. Danny broke his arm, his friend was crippled, his fiancée ran away, and he lost his ever-after dream. There was no football, no marriage, no dream life. His chest still burned with bitterness on occasion.

He leaned back on the bench and closed his eyes. The bloody scene of Paul and him at the bottom of the concrete stairs wasn't there. No screams. No blood. No pain.

That awfulness was replaced with another vision. One he'd seen at dawn. It was Andi standing in the huge cabin window totally nude. Her eyes were closed. He didn't turn away, he just stared. She was smiling at the night. Her hair hung wet down to her waist. No painting could match the beauty.

Danny had felt the earth shift as dawn's light moved over her. He was changing, scars and all. He felt something for the first time in years, hurting, aware, alive. This ornery, bossy, headstrong woman was pulling him out of the fog and making him breathe whether he wanted to or not.

Chapter 9

Noah's Doubts

Friday

As Noah did every night, he closed the bookshop at six o'clock and walked across to the café. There was a round table near the front door for men eating supper alone. The unmarried, the widowers, the traveling truckers who knew the food was good, but the people who interested him most were the bewildered husbands.

Mateo, the café's owner, didn't want a table taken up by one man so he always herded the lonely to the first big round table. The men didn't seem to mind eating with strangers since Mateo offered a free dessert.

The women always came in groups to eat. They ate further inside the café where the wind didn't bother them every time the door opened. Noah noticed none of the women even glanced at the round table of men. He figured that table was the leftovers, like the "last chance" bin at the dollar store. At even half price no one wanted them.

The last kind of men to find a seat at the table were the bewildered husbands, who didn't talk much. They just ate or cried or cussed, usually without following the conversation.

Eventually they'd start talking. They all had the same story. It started with something simple. He forgot an anniversary, or a birthday, or a dinner with her parents. He'd say he was tired or worked late to explain calling it an early night. He'd just say he didn't want to talk about it.

She'd forgive him once, but the game was on.

Strike one.

Then after a month or so he'd stop to have a beer with the guys and forget to call. After all, he'd say, he's an adult. He didn't need a leash; he'd declare she was nagging while he ate his cold, leftover supper.

Strike two.

Then he stopped talking to the wife, and just argued. Any room and subject was fair game.

Then came the next mistake—he swore it wasn't his fault. He hadn't been thinking straight. He didn't mean to sleep with another woman; it just happened.

Strike three.

Before he knew it, his clothes were on the lawn and now he's sitting at the single man table at Mateo's.

The interesting thing about it to Noah was they each thought that it's all their wives' or girlfriends' fault. She wasn't fair. No one was perfect. He'd never do it again, he swore.

The other men at the table with the homeless husband agreed it wasn't fair. After all, he'd made it home 364 days out of 365, and he swore he had no idea where his underwear was.

Noah never said a word. Sometimes the bewildered guy hammered the last nail in his own coffin. He told the wife that the woman wasn't even good-looking or good at sex most of the time.

About then the wife screamed, or worse, stomped on his best hat lying in the grass. Now and then the guy's head was in it.

Noah took notes, but he'd never been dumped. He'd never even been in love, or talked to anyone he didn't have to. He remembered his mother telling him to not talk to the other kids in grade school. By high school most of the kids already had their friends, so he walked the halls alone. Not even the bullies bothered to pick on him. In college most of his dates were study dates or blind dates that neither wanted to repeat.

The one relationship he could remember was his parents'. But it was largely a silent partnership. He never remembered any real affection between them and very little conversation. He didn't remember them arguing or fighting, all he remembered was the silence. He found it both frightening and comforting at the same time. It was one of the reasons that the tales these men had of passionate outbursts and all-night arguments with their spouses fascinated him. He couldn't imagine such a life and wondered what the children in those households remembered. It was as if there was so much more to grasp about the way men and women loved one another, and even though these tales largely ended the same way—badly—it set his imagination on fire. How could you love someone so much and yet hurt them so easily? Love, like everything else in Noah's life, was something he viewed from the sidelines and not something he really experienced himself.

As he left the café, Noah thought he might be turning into one of the locals, even though he couldn't say "Howdy" right. He'd started talking about what he wanted to do someday, but he never took one step toward those goals, like taking a road trip some summer. Paint the bookshop. Run for mayor, even though he'd never have a chance, not being born and raised here. If your mother didn't spill her birthing blood in the county, you'd always be an outsider.

When he'd leased the bookshop, he'd told himself he'd close the place and take a vacation for a month every year. He'd buy posters from every place he went and plaster the walls of his apartment. He'd fly to New York most Christmases and see his folks and go to a Broadway play every night. Then he'd come back and tell these Texans what it was like. He might play all the songs of the plays in the shop, whether he had time to see the shows or not.

Some nights, goals filled his thoughts as Noah talked to the stars. He'd tell the moon he'd learn something new every season. He'd promised himself he'd not just dream; he'd do. He wanted to discover things. Wander out of his quiet, comfortable life.

He'd almost done that last summer. He stepped out of his comfort zone to have an adventure. He got to the door of the bar in Clifton Bend. The college town was lively. But when the bar's door opened, he saw kids ten years younger stomping to country music. He'd tried another bar in Someday Valley. He made it not more than three feet inside when he decided the music was too loud and the room too crowded. Then it got worse when they locked arms over each other in a row and all yelled "Bull shit!" Two words seemed to be the limit of the lyrics.

Noah grinned thinking these cowboys were the worst imitation in the world of the Rockettes. One three-hundred-pound drunk tripped over his boots and took half the line dancers to the floor.

Noah had chuckled as he drove straight home, parked in front of his bookshop and promised himself he'd give up on living the wild life. A blink later he was running past his apartment on the second floor and heading for the roof. He'd climbed the stairs two at a time until he reached his destination. He stood on the edge at the back of the building, looked down at the dark water below and yelled, "Bull shit!" for no reason at all.

Noah had walked out of the bar thinking living life full-out wasn't as fun as he thought it might be. He wanted to take big bites of life, but all he ever got were hors d'oeuvres.

Tonight, months since he'd tried to live one adventure, he

stood alone in the cold of midnight, then paced the roof of the mall and took a deep breath. Sometimes being with people was lonelier than standing alone. Maybe he should just stay on the roof until he starved or got lucky and lightning struck him.

Suddenly his primal cry for answers echoed off the night. All the notes he'd written about the locals not following their dreams didn't mean anything. He wasn't making notes about others; he was writing about himself. His parents were right. If he didn't set goals, draw a map, climb every mountain, push, and push, and push, he'd get nowhere.

He had less money today than when he left New York. He hadn't visited any of the places he'd dreamed of going. Not one poster was on his wall. He had no friends. No girlfriend or a sometime lover. Not even one who would kick him out because he was nothing.

Looking over the little town, Noah realized Honey Creek was as beautiful as always, but he didn't belong here.

He belonged nowhere.

A low voice floating on the breeze almost seemed real. "Are you all right, Noah?"

He didn't move. "Great, now I'm hearing things. I'm not a failure; I'm just going crazy. If you don't mind, I think I'll fall apart alone."

The light laughter he'd heard twice before reached his ears more like a memory than reality as he slowly turned around.

Cora Lee, the silent daughter of Bear Buchanan, seemed to materialize out of the shadows. "You all right, Mr. O'Brien?" she asked again.

"I don't know. I think I'm having a breakdown. Of course, if I did crack up, I'd be doing something new. Every day is the same. Nothing changes. Insanity is riding this merry-go-round I'm on and I have no clue how to get off."

He heard that gentle laugh again. "No, you're not. I teach first grade. Believe me, I know the difference between a breakdown and a fit. A breakdown is usually when you're carrying too much on your shoulders. Too many bills or problems or even too many kids mobbing you in the hallway.

"When someone has a breakdown, they don't think they can handle it all. A fit is when you don't get what you want and everyone around you has to deal with it."

He smiled. She had never had a conversation more than two sentences with him, and here she was analyzing his problem. He felt like a fool.

He wouldn't have thought he could feel any lower tonight, but she managed the task. "I'm all right. I just cracked for a minute. I'll get over it, Miss Buchanan."

She put her fists on her hips and said in her teacher voice, "Tell me what has you so upset. You're a good man, Mr. O'Brien. No matter what monster you are fighting, I'll help you. After eight years of teaching first-graders, I can handle any crisis."

With the shadows of night almost swallowing her, he faced her and realized this shy woman was a beautiful warrior. Her kids must love her. She was standing in front of him ready to help him fight the demons she couldn't even see.

For the first time Noah wanted to open up to someone. No, that's not right. He wanted to open up to her.

He pulled up a decrepit lawn chair he sometimes sat in to watch the stars. But tonight, he offered it to her as he leaned against the three-foot roof border that fenced them in like a crown atop the mall.

As midnight crawled toward them, the town settled down to sleep. No cars passing. No barking dogs. No people chatting below on the town square. He talked, but all he heard was the water splashing nearby.

His words moved slowly and lowered. He could see the moon's glow in her eyes and for a moment he wondered if she was real. A listener found by a man who never truly talked. Noah began by telling her about growing up and being a lonely only child. He never remembered his parents playing a board game with him, or taking him to a show or even a vacation.

He described middle school, where he thought he was invisible, and high school, when he wished he could be. The few times he asked to go to a dance or a ballgame, his father would remind him there were more important things to do.

For the past three years he'd held inside all of his thoughts and his opinions. Never talking between all the "Good mornings" and "I think you'll like this new release." He had a thousand nothing words to say: *Have a great day. Come back. Good to see you again.*

Words that passed between people that meant zero.

As he looked out at the stream, he realized he'd talked to the water more than any person in town.

When he glanced back, Noah could almost see behind Cora Lee's eyes. A loneliness was there that mirrored his own. A loneliness he knew well. A watcher. Never an adventurer. Her big sister did all the talking and all the living. Cora Lee was the follower, the listener.

"You'll be all right, Noah. Lonely will pass," she said as if she knew the place called Lonely well.

Her shy smile slowly returned. "What would you want to do, Mr. O'Brien, right now? Would you run away from Honey Creek like you did from New York? Would you jump off the roof to see if you could fly? Would you laugh at the world and turn away from people like I sometimes do?"

She raised her arms. "Fog is coming in. No one will see you. What do you wish you could do?"

He took a step closer and realized she was the sister that no one saw. Kind, bright, and full of empathy.

One thought filled his mind. It wasn't about him or his problems. The adventure he was looking for might just be getting to understand Cora Lee.

His words were low, flowing on the wind. "I'd kiss you if I could do anything."

The words were out before he could stop them. It seemed for once in his life he said exactly what he thought . . . what he wanted.

Her green eyes widened as she stepped back and he realized she was going to take flight.

"I'm . . . Oh, Miss Buchanan, I'm sorry . . . I hope I didn't offend you. I . . . I . . ." Noah was taking more time apologizing than he'd taken in asking. She'd been the one who inquired what he wanted to do and all he'd done was answer honestly.

Noah realized he was identifying with the bewildered husbands at the café. He couldn't understand.

He looked down at her braided hair. He knew she was almost as old as he was, but the braids made her look younger.

Noah had to convince her he wasn't nuts. "I'm sorry. I . . ." No more words came. He wished he could disappear. Or maybe he should tell her to vanish. After all, he was on the roof first. She'd be mad and never talk to him again.

To his surprise, she took a step toward him.

Noah did his best to turn to stone. Anything else was bound to be the wrong move.

She looked directly at him. "Mr. O'Brien, if you wish to kiss me, I have no objection. It's been a long time since anyone kissed me."

Her words were so unexpected they almost felt like a slap.

"Are you sure? I don't want to make you uncomfortable because I asked. I . . ."

She smiled that shy smile again. "I'm not a child. I know my own mind. At this rate, it will be dawn before you move. Your suggestion was interesting."

Both seemed to stop even breathing.

Finally, she looked up. "Yes, Mr. O'Brien, I'd like you to kiss me. If we don't like the exchange, we'll never mention it again."

Noah took a step toward her. He still wanted to kiss her, but she seemed to take it as a dare.

She lifted her head up as he moved closer. One inch apart. She didn't look afraid or even interested.

"Close your eyes." He expected her to argue, but she didn't.

Slowly he pulled the rubber band from the end of her braid and freed her hair. One side, then the other. It was thick and felt like satin.

She didn't move and she didn't follow orders. She just stared at him as if she could read his mind.

The breeze blew a strand across her face and he gently brushed it away. When his fingers moved a curl back into place, his thumb brushed over her lips and she finally closed her eyes.

She swayed a bit and he put his arm around her and pulled her closer. "This is going to take some time. Any objection?"

"No," she answered as his lips touched hers.

He'd meant to go slow, but suddenly the desire to connect pushed them both forward. He pulled her against his chest and laced his fingers into her hair. He could feel her heart pounding, but she didn't remain still. She wrapped her arms around his neck as if she was holding on to life.

The kiss was tender for a moment, then both grew hungry for more.

He feared he was hugging her too tightly. Bruising her lips. He wanted to slow down. She was fragile and he shouldn't hold her too close, but when he tried to slow, she wouldn't let him. They were both starving.

Two lonely people, he thought. Two lost souls afraid to live. Two hearts craving connection.

Suddenly, he realized his heart had shattered. The feelings inside him might last a second or a lifetime, but he couldn't have stopped if the whole town was watching. For a breath she was against him. Heart against heart.

As the full moon passed over the sky, they slowed. He picked up Cora and moved to the old lawn chair. He sat down and she cuddled in his arms as if she belonged there. With their cheeks almost touching they watched the stars peeking between clouds.

He slid his hands along her arms and then her back and finally along her legs. *You're real*, he almost said out loud.

When he pushed the hem of her skirt a few inches above her knee she said softly, "You mind if I touch you as well? I have to believe you're authentic and not a strange ghost dressed as my bookshop owner. I'd be kissing an imposter wearing my Noah's glasses."

He stilled, then slowly leaned down as his forehead touched hers. "So, I'm your Noah?"

"Yes. You have been for a while. You are kind and smart. I just didn't know how to tell you. If you want to be mine for while?"

"Makes more sense than you thinking I'm one of the long-dead spirits from the third floor." He felt her laughter against his chest. "If I'm yours for a moment, would it be all right if you're mine?"

He brushed her hair from her cheek and wished they'd stay close for a while. He wanted to hold her, kiss her again, and talk to her.

To his surprise she cuddled against him and he knew she'd felt lonely to the bone. They both had lived without companionship or touch for so long.

He held her hands and tried to think of something, anything to say.

"What's up on the third floor?" he asked as he thought it was a dumb thing to say but he had to talk. "I've thought of searching for a desk to use downstairs. It wouldn't be stealing. I'm not taking it out of the building."

Cora giggled and her breath brushed his throat. "There is nothing important in there. Just junk. I remember three other businesses on the first floor before you came." Her words came low and almost disappeared on the wind.

They were talking of nothing but the brush of her cheek against his was communicating and the light movement of his hand along her back was answering.

Her words whispered against his ear. "Once it was a children's bookshop with toys among secondhand books. The old lady who ran it promised to come back for the toys, but she didn't. She wrote Bear and told him to give the books to the library. My dad is still storing the old toys for her, even though she'd be a hundred by now.

"Then, there was an antique store. The guy who ran it, a World War One vet, was older than any of the furniture he tried to sell, but he told everyone he'd be rich soon.

"He died and his kids, long grown, said they would pick up the inventory. But it has been decades since they buried the old guy, and the heirs should be old enough to drive by now." She tried to hide her amusement at her joke.

Moving her hand across his chest she lowered her words, "I like being close to you. You feel very real. Sometimes, when Kat and I are having coffee, I think you're vanishing. You're like me, one of the people others don't notice."

His reply was lost in her kiss.

The feel of her skin warmed him as he kissed across her cheek. "I love this, but is it too much too fast, Miss Buchanan?"

He felt her laugh against his forehead as he moved to kiss her throat. Noah loved that he could feel her emotions as well as hear them.

She pulled away a few inches and he felt the night's cold. Her fists were back on her waist. The teacher was back. "All right. I liked the kiss and you holding me, but you've got to stop calling me Miss Buchanan."

"What should I call you? Cora or Cora Lee?"

She kissed the tip of his nose. "I don't know. You ask too many questions. Can we go back to kissing?"

"So, you do like my kiss?" He felt like a kid.

She rested her cheek on his chest and answered, "I'm not

sure, Mr. O'Brien. I feel like I might have another taste if you don't mind."

Without a word his kiss turned light and tender. He didn't care what he called her and she could call him anything she wanted to when they were in public as long as he could kiss her now and then.

He decided he'd always call her "Dear" in his mind, and hopefully when they were alone.

Whether they lasted a day, a month, or a lifetime, he'd never forget this night. He'd always thought love slammed into people. But it didn't. It drifted in, as if it had been there all the time.

This night, three years after he settled in the valley, he had his first grand adventure. Tonight, he'd come alive.

An hour later, the wind was blowing in a cold front and they rushed to the roof door. They held hands as they walked down.

In the hallway light, she was back to being shy. He let go of her hand.

She backed away as if they were simply strangers passing on the steps.

"What's wrong?" He slowed.

She moved away another few inches. "I'm sorry, Noah. It's just been a long time since I've been kissed and never like you just did. I have no idea what to say. *Thank you* doesn't seem right."

Every cell inside him wanted to feel her against him. He'd gone beyond just a kiss. He wanted to pull her into his arms. But he might frighten her. He couldn't order her to kiss him again and he couldn't walk away.

When they stood still, a breath between them in the dark, dusty hallway, he was afraid to push her into something he wasn't sure she could handle.

She wasn't looking up at him. Strangers again, he feared.

He had to let her know how he felt. He wanted to tell her how much this moment meant.

He took a step away. "Are you all right, Cora Lee?"

She nodded but still didn't look at him. He couldn't let it end like this.

"Miss Buchanan, would you allow me to kiss you goodnight now and then? Seems everyone in the world has someone to kiss, and you're the only one I want to."

She nodded again without looking up.

Noah pulled a rag from his back pocket that he used to wipe dust off the tables. He raised it and unscrewed the stairway lightbulb. Then, slowly he leaned down and kissed her cheek as they stood in shadow.

"Again?" he whispered in her ear.

She nodded.

He kissed her lightly again, barely touching her lips, but his hands circled her waist and tugged her closer. "I want you near me. If you object, you'd best say so. I'd like to get closer every time I see you. I want you against me so I can match my breathing to yours."

When he straightened and took one step away, he waited for her to react. After a very long moment, she looked up. "Again?"

"Of course, dear."

This time she moved toward him and he wrapped his arms around her. For a while all he wanted to do was learn how she wanted to be kissed. Every time he got it just right, he heard a little sound that made him smile.

When he finally pulled an inch away, he said, "You all right with this?

. . . with us?"

"Yes." Her fingers fisted in his sweater as if she'd never allow him to leave.

"Me too, but don't worry; we'll go slow. I don't want to frighten you. I'll make sure you're all right with everything. We've got all the time in the world. We'll talk and get to know each other. We may have to give your father time to get used to me being around you. I waited a year for Bear to smile at me. I'll be near retirement before he slaps me on the back."

To his surprise she put her fingers over his lips. "Stop. I have to tell you something."

"All right." A dozen things went through his mind. She probably wanted to tell him this was a one-time thing. It would never happen again. She's dying and can't get mixed up with him. She was moving to another country. She didn't really like him. She had another lover and didn't have time. She's joining a nunnery. He kissed too bad to try again.

"What? Tell me." He stepped away. Whatever came might feel like a blow.

He could almost feel her green eyes staring at him for a moment before she said, "I don't want to go slow."

He fought for air.

She simply smiled, kissed him on his cheek, and said, "We'll have coffee in the morning and work out the details."

When she turned and went inside her apartment, Noah stood in the dark hallway. For a moment he didn't know where he was. What floor, what building, what town, what planet.

"Goodnight!" he yelled loud enough to wake the ghosts on the third floor.

Then, he remembered. He was alive.

Chapter 10

Andi's Hideout

Cloudy Saturday afternoon

Andi Delane was dressed in jeans and an orange sweatshirt with GO COYOTES across her chest when the deputy knocked on the cabin door.

He straightened to full attention as if making a formal call. "Morning, ma'am. I wasn't sure you'd be here. I was called into the office to be briefed."

She managed a quick smile as she lied. "I try to be truthful, Deputy. If I say I'll be somewhere, I will. Besides, I have a tell when I lie." Andi moved back into the cabin to pick up her jacket. "If you ever discover it, you'll be able to read me."

Andi watched him as he told her he'd left a twig in the tiny crack between the door and the frame. "If you'd opened the door one inch, I would have known you went out. If the twig had fallen, I'd know someone tried the lock while you slept."

"Thanks for telling me, Deputy. I found the twig ten minutes after you left. I set a few traps, if anyone tries to bother me. I appreciate you watching over me, just don't get in my way. I'm used to working alone."

For a few minutes they just stood there at the door staring at one another. She noted the facts. Tall, muscles from working at something other than investigating, she guessed. Hair more rust colored than red. Gave off a nonchalant attitude but watched everything. She had thought he was a complete doofus at first, an easy assessment. But she'd also learned how deceiving first impressions could be. It was one thing she was very careful about when in deep cover, to keep reinforcing those initial perceptions to prevent perps from reassessing her. Even though this was a small town, there was no such thing as too careful. He might give off dumb jock vibes, but she suspected there might be more under the surface.

As she kept studying the deputy, she felt a sadness about him. For once he wasn't smiling his happy-go-lucky smile. She told herself she didn't believe in aura, but she did trust her gut, and this morning it sensed a sorrow, a loss so deep she wanted to know more, to reach out.

I'm cracking up, she almost said aloud. Andi never, never, reached out to people. Maybe it was better if she knew nothing about the deputy's thoughts and simply focused on facts.

The deputy looked nervous. She hadn't asked him in and she didn't close the door in his face. It was like life had stopped for a second but her brain was still firing.

She pointed to the porch chair. "I won't be long. I have research to finish." Leaving the door open, she turned and walked back in, watching him in the mirror on the opposite wall above the recliner.

The deputy seemed to have some trouble getting comfortable in an old chair on the porch that needed to be turned into firewood. "It's a bit cool out here," he grumbled.

A blanket flew through the open door and landed on his chest, and he spread it over himself. He was quiet while she typed and cussed silently. Frustration grew as the computer misspelled word after word. Her focus was clearly not what it should be this morning. She called the device several creative names, but it still refused to work right. She cursed under her breath every time she had to backspace and try again.

His words came softly. "I worried about you out here. You're tall, but you'd be no match for a bar fighter. And from your cussing you're losing that fight with the laptop."

"Thanks for sharing," she said between silent cusswords. "But you can rest easy; I'm well-armed."

"I know you're armed and aware of how alone you are out here."

"Right," she said and smiled in spite of her irritation at the computer.

He straightened and watched her directly. "You're clearly not a criminal, but the sheriff talks about you like you're made of glass, which is the direct opposite of what I'm seeing. No one in the office is allowed to ask, or answer, questions about you. The sheriff doesn't even talk to the Texas Ranger who revolves through our back door like he's welcome." The deputy paused his monologue.

Without a word she stood and walked out of his sight and over to the bed. Andi buckled her customized duty belt around her waist. It was a special stripped-down version for undercover work, with a small flashlight on one side and a hunting knife on the other. It molded to her form over her jeans and was well covered by the Clifton College sweatshirt she'd bought in the bookshop. It's not that his words made her nervous, but it was more the fact that an easygoing place like Honey Creek could lull anyone into complacency. Knowing these tools were within her grasp was a reminder that things were never as calm or simple as they seemed.

She glanced toward the porch and couldn't resist goading him a bit. "A few more hours and we can get some food, maybe."

He growled as he tried to get comfortable and she fought down a giggle. The big guy was so completely real. In her world of fake identities and lying criminals, it was a nice change and one she was starting to get used to. Part of her liked the fact that this was one person who was what he was, all the time, every day. A little piece of her wondered what it might be like to live in a world of real, honest people again. It was attractive and a little scary. Even honest people can disappoint you and she knew better than to open herself up to someone, anyone, so completely. She'd been there before. Still, this place fit like a well-worn shoe. Comfortable, welcoming, and easy.

She worked while the deputy slept on the cabin porch like a protective Rottweiler.

Two hours passed with lightning speed as she searched for anything to lead her to her brothers or tell her more about the man that fathered them all. She read town histories, searched local family trees, and even looked through online cemetery records trying to connect people together. While she didn't find much about Morrell, she did learn that the people of this whole area were woven together like thin strands of a spider's web. They were either directly related, related by marriage, or offspring of hookups and poor decisions. It was good information, as it was clear that any poking around that was not done carefully would be town gossip in hours, if not minutes.

There was movement on the porch and Andi grinned to herself as the deputy woke, roared like a hungry bear, and poked his head into her one-room cabin. "I kept you safe as promised. Now are we gonna eat?"

She looked at him a moment and thought. From what she'd learned, the gossip wagon was probably already trying to figure out who she was. Some kind of believable cover story, within the sheriff's department at least, seemed prudent. No information was worse than some information, even if it wasn't exactly true. She quickly improvised something believable.

"To answer some of the questions I'm sure you have, Deputy, I'm actually a pilot hired by the Dallas PD. Mostly I make maps over rough land or fly some big shot to a meeting. I

don't tell people where I'm headed. It's safer for me and them."
She lifted one eyebrow as she watched him take in every word.
The job description wasn't quite accurate, but it was just
enough to dull the roar of questions that swirled around. "Because of my job I stay on alert. There are a few bad guys who'd
pay money to know my flight plan or get to people that I'm
transporting."

She hesitated, allowing that information to sink in, and
could tell the deputy believed the story. She might need this
man's help at some point, so creating an ally was critical.

"I never fly around here because this valley doesn't have an
airstrip."

"A few months ago, I was spotted somewhere by the wrong
people. I reported it to my supervisor. He said for me to stay
out of that region for a while. Then a man, who shouldn't even
be in the States, was arrested. He had a photo of me in his
pocket. It was grainy but it was me, and that's how we learned
there's a price on my head."

The deputy stepped back as she walked out on the porch
and turned toward him, leaning back on the railing. "Most of
the time my job is boring, but now and then I fly into a place
where criminals don't want company. It's usually best if I'm
just a ghost passing by. I get out of danger as fast as I can."

She smiled a sad smile. "This isn't where I want to be right
now, but I'm grateful for a place to hide out and stay off the
grid until things blow over. So far, I have to say the town and
the welcome"—she motioned to him—"has been top-notch."

"I understand. I'll keep that information private; you can
rest assured. It also lets me know how serious the threat is and
that we really need to be as aware as possible." He crossed his
arms and met her gaze with solid confidence. "I appreciate you
trusting me."

She nodded as if they'd just shared their deepest secrets, but
she knew that too much information wouldn't help either one
of them, so giving just enough was the right move.

Pop told her once that she had an ear for the truth and because of that, she knew how the truth sounded and how to create full confidence in another person that her words were real. In deep cover you had to tell believable lies and she was very good at it. From the time she was a child, Andi could accurately read people and it still amazed her how many people didn't have that same skill, especially in law enforcement. The deputy seemed to be one of those rare souls who assumed people were mostly good, or at least well intentioned, and the others were just misguided.

The deputy waited as she grabbed her jacket.

"You think you could call me Danny or even Dan?" he asked with a smile. "We're going to be spending a lot of time together and we ought to be on a first-name basis. Especially if I'm going to be Festus to your Marshal Dillon."

She looked at him, confused.

"You know, *Gunsmoke*."

"What is *Gunsmoke*?"

He shook his head as she walked in front of him and down the steps. "Bless your heart, girl. How could you not know *Gunsmoke*? My grandpa has every episode ever made. Had me convert eighty-four old VHS tapes so he could still watch them. When I was a kid, I thought the actors were my relatives because we talked about them so often." He grinned. "I'll download a few episodes and bring them by for you to watch."

"Okay, thanks. Let's go get some lunch." She couldn't have cared less about some old Western show, but if that was part of creating an ally then so be it. The deputy double-checked that the cabin door was locked securely and reset his twig trap, then got into the truck with her.

Andi said, "I also need to talk to you about that idea you had last night."

"What idea?" He backed the truck out of the campground and headed toward the center of town. "I don't remember many ideas lately. I average four hours of sleep after following you around, and in my sleep, I'm usually guarding you."

Andi noticed one side of his hair was sticking straight up. She had to fight the urge to push it down.

Bad idea. Don't get too close.

Half the time she wanted to slug him for tailing her so obviously, but she had to remember that she needed allies, not friends. *Stay on point*, she reminded herself.

"The idea you had about me being your girlfriend, Deputy. I mean, Danny. That might be a good cover. It would explain why we are always together." She plunged into her reasoning before he asked too many questions. "Unless we want the gossip to get out of hand, we need something plausible. If they see us together, eating, riding around town or whatever, I think it's much better to say we are old friends that are dating rather than them make up wild stories."

She stared at his errant hair while he processed what she was saying. She thought a moment. "We knew each other at Texas Tech. Noah told me you went there. Around here it's a good idea to know the school song. Alumni tend to break out in song when they meet."

Danny propped one elbow up on the open window of the truck and rubbed a finger across his chin, thinking it through. Finally, he said, "You're right about the gossip in this town; it makes 'might have' into 'probably a fact' lightning fast. Truth rattles around on the country roads. Just the number of reports we get of someone scratching their own car door is nuts."

Andi frowned. *What?* She doubted the people here were that crazy, but whatever. She could see him getting on board with this idea.

"I appreciate you considering it. Now that you know how vital it is that I lay low, you know it's not just a game we are playing."

"Understood. I can certainly play the part of an old friend, or even boyfriend if you like, and people in town might be a bit more friendly toward you."

Andi breathed a sigh of relief. There was now no time to waste with the second part of her plan. From her research, she knew this deputy's family roots ran deep in the whole area and he could be very helpful getting the information she had been searching for.

"One other thing you should know. I chose to come to Honey Creek because apparently my real father, who I never met, is from here. The lawyer called my mother and told her he had died and that I had brothers. I thought that would be a good excuse to hide out here instead of somewhere else. I'd like to find those brothers if possible."

Danny rubbed his chin again. "Who was your dad?"

"Not dad really, more like sperm donor."

The deputy grinned and she smiled back. This was going well. "Jamie Morrell."

He frowned. "Hmm. Jamie Morrell. It doesn't ring a bell right off, but I'll think on it and ask around a bit."

"I'd appreciate it." Andi reminded herself to remain stoic, but she was thrilled at how easily he agreed to everything.

She looked at his solid, muscular frame. "What about pretending we are a couple? Do you really think you can do it?"

"I can pull it off, of course." He raised a skeptical brow. "But not sure you can. No one will believe we are a couple if you keep treating me like a brainless chump."

Andi stilled. She hadn't been vigilant enough, big mistake. She studied him out of the corner of her eye as he focused on the road. The deputy didn't play himself up, but she caught him logging everything he saw or heard. She always prided herself on being the smartest person in the room, not only because her life depended on it, but because she could accurately read everyone else's motives. Had he guessed hers?

She chose a different angle. "Well, clearly you were a jock in high school and I'll admit I didn't have many deep conversations with those types back in the day."

He smiled. "People can surprise you."

Not likely. She blew it off and refused to be rattled. "Well, if you don't think it's believable that you'd be dating someone like me, then we can rethink it."

"I don't know if that is an insult or a compliment." He pushed back his hat and dug fingers through his sunshine-red hair. "Let me be sure I have your story straight."

The way he said the word *story* got another glance from Andi.

"You came to Honey Creek to lay low because some bad guy put a price on your head. So now, because you don't have anything to do, you plan to find brothers you don't even know?" He looked at her again.

"Well, yeah. That's how it has worked out."

Moments ticked by as he slid the hat back into place and pulled up to the café. "I can toe that line for a while."

Andi's gut flashed warning signs. She'd had less trouble convincing cartel chiefs she was on their side. She was definitely losing her touch if she couldn't convince one mid-level deputy in Tiny Town USA.

She wondered at his hesitancy. "Don't tell me you already have a girlfriend or a wife. That will kill the plan."

"No. No girlfriend or wife, not even a woman who talks to me on a regular basis. So, the problem isn't me so much as it is the perception in town that I don't date."

"Why? Are girls not your thing?"

They sat in the silent truck a moment as the deputy turned a stone face in her direction. "Lady, you're the one asking for my help and I don't appreciate women who manipulate and push people's buttons to get their way, understand?"

His tone shivered up her spine and gave her the idea this guy had a real bad-ass side he rarely showed. She went into professional cop mode. "Got it. My apologies, Deputy. How do you want to proceed?"

He opened his door and looked at her. "Follow my lead and don't act stupid." He got out and headed to the sidewalk.

Andi almost kicked her door open. The nerve of this guy. In no way did she put him in charge of this little theater act, and who was he, of all people, to tell her not to act stupid? As far as she could see, he'd pretty much cornered the market on that. She marched up to him as he put a hand on the café door. Her head leaned back to allow him full view of her withering glare.

"Now remember to smile, sweet pea." He grinned and opened the door, firmly guiding her forward with a beefy hand on her back.

Dan hesitated for a moment to allow his eyes to adjust to the café interior and then followed Andi to an open table. He set his hat on an empty chair and grabbed a menu from the center of the table. Andi followed suit. A fifty-something waitress with glasses and short salt-and-pepper curls quickly appeared and grinned at him. "Well, what do we have here, Dan?" She looked at Andi.

He gave her a big goofy smile. "Just an old friend from college, Betty. Wanted to bring her by for a real green-chile cheeseburger." He motioned across the table. "This is Andi."

Andi nodded at the waitress. "Nice to meet you."

They quickly ordered and Dan could tell there was still a little steam coming off Andi's face from their exchange in the truck. Good. She deserved it. She'd been downright nasty since he'd started tailing her, and he had discovered that getting under her skin was more fun than expected. Sure, she was hot, but she knew it too and used it effectively, and that was not exactly attractive. However, seeing her riled up made his heart beat triple time, and what was the harm in that?

He wasn't quite sure what her game was, but this little turn of events was interesting. He had to watch her either way and this way was a lot more fun, not to mention the fact he got to eat on a regular basis.

"So"—he smiled at Andi's clenched teeth and lowered his voice—"I have to tell you I'm not a pro at dating. Haven't done it for a long time."

"You don't say." Sarcasm dripped off her words.

"I know it's hard to believe," he continued as if clueless to her irritation, "but it's true. I seem to struggle to figure out what makes women happy."

"Shocking."

"I guess my real skill is pissing them off; that I'm really good at that."

"You seem so proud." Her lips drew into a thin, tight smile.

He shrugged as their iced tea arrived. "It's a gift I think."

He could almost feel the eye roll as he took a big gulp of tea. It occurred to him this could be the highlight of his year, so why not just go with it? She'd treated him like he was stupid from the first second, so playing that role had come easy. No reason not to, she'd be gone soon anyway, and it was better than writing reports.

They sat in silence for a while and Dan glanced around the café. It was clear they were the center of attention. "This little act isn't gonna fly if you sit there angry and pouting the whole time we eat."

After lunch, Dan paid at the counter. When he saw her frown, he said, "You can get the next bill if you like, but I don't mind picking up the tab. After all, you are my date."

She started to argue but then stopped. If they were playing this game in front of the town, they might as well make it look real.

He slipped his arm around her shoulder and looked down at her as if he'd just ordered dessert.

She smiled as she circled his waist. Nothing personal, just part of the game.

Dan noticed a light honeysuckle scent rose from her hair that tickled his chin while the rest of her body fit right into his. He'd never held a tall woman this close and had to admit it was fantastic. She was slender, but strong.

A teen rushed past Andi with a bump.

Dan pulled her a few inches closer.

"Sorry," the kid yelled to apologize to Andi as he pulled the door open. "I'll be late to class."

Andi smiled. "No harm done."

The teen glanced up at Dan's frown and quickly disappeared.

Dan loosened his grip on her. "You okay?"

"Yep." She slid to the side and grabbed his arm, and they walked out together looking very much like a couple.

Her touch on his bicep was feather soft, but he felt every single nerve cell firing. His skin tremored involuntarily, and he hoped she didn't notice. He opened the truck's passenger door and her hand slid from his arm and down his back a short distance as she got into the truck. The firestorm across his skin was like a lightning bolt and he breathed deep, trying to calm his racing thoughts as he walked around the truck and climbed in.

This is never going to work, he said to himself. Playing this game was the most frightening thing he'd done in three years.

They rode in uncomfortable silence until they arrived back at the cabin. Dan turned the engine off, and Andi smiled a little but didn't look at him.

Dan waited a moment in silence, then said, "Sorry if I overstepped a little back in the café."

She didn't say a word.

He tried again. "I guess I'm not used to being touched or touching anyone. When the kid ran into you, I may have overreacted."

No reason not to admit it, he decided. "I guess I'm a born protector."

"Noted." She climbed out of the truck, walked toward the porch, unlocked the cabin, and disappeared. No comment.

Dan sat in the quiet for a minute wondering if maybe, just maybe, he'd bitten off more than he could chew this time.

With his luck, Dan wouldn't figure Andi out before he was to date for real.

It occurred to him that maybe he should protect himself from her. She seemed to be made of steel.

A grin spread across his face as he remembered the fire that shot through him when she was against him for a moment.

No doubt. He was the moth and she was the light. He'd be careful or he'd be burned, and at this point he didn't care.

Chapter 11

First Pretend Date

Saturday

They'd discussed the particulars yesterday, down to every detail. Andi's idea was to see and be seen with the deputy in a way that would allow them to talk to as many people as possible. He had agreed and said Saturday in town would be the easiest day to see a good cross section of people who might remember Jamie Morrell.

Andi knew it was a long shot they'd find anyone willing to talk about her father, but it was a chance.

They were both dressed casually. The deputy had ditched his uniform and dressed in a T-shirt and jeans. The denim jacket and old straw hat made him look more like a farmer than any kind of law enforcement.

She had to take a second look when he walked up. The T-shirt showed off his muscles. He looked homegrown and model tan.

Andi had donned jeans and another sweatshirt from her small Clifton Bend collection. Her leather jacket was simple, but warm.

The deputy parked his farm pickup near her cabin. It was an older Ford that looked as if it had been well used over the years. It would give any passerby the idea the cabin was occupied.

As they headed down the trail to town, Andi could admit she was a little nervous. Being seen as a couple in a lunchtime café was one thing, but in plain view of the whole town, there was no going back.

From the moment they walked out of the trees the picture-perfect view of the little town welcomed her.

Andi wondered if the locals even noticed what beauty surrounded them.

As they walked across the square, she smiled thinking about the game they were playing and knew the best course of action was to lean into it and make it as real as possible. They had to be a sweet couple, laughing and flirting as would be expected. It was a very different role than she usually played undercover, but there was no reason not to enjoy it.

Maybe it would take her mind off her troubles. A few people dotted the sidewalks as they neared; she could almost hear the director yell, *Action!* Andi wrapped her hand around Danny's upper arm, squeezing near his muscular form and smiling up at him. In silhouette the deputy was almost handsome. Tall, but in a just-the-right-size way for her, and built of rock with a low, almost sultry voice that was not hard to listen to.

He fit the strong, law enforcement stereotype, unfortunately, and she'd had quite enough of that with Texas Ranger Carl Ramm. It wasn't that those types weren't good men, they were. They tended to be polite and gentle to most everyone, until you disagreed with them or their ideas. Then, it was a nonnegotiable line in the sand. No give, no gray area, no discussion. While this deputy was no Carl Ramm, she had seen a small idea of what he might be like when crossed, and it certainly fit the mold.

The good thing about that was that it made it very easy for her to keep some healthy emotional distance. She didn't follow anyone's rules but her own when it came to her life, and she certainly wasn't going to be ordered around in any relationship. No matter how good it might look at first, it just wasn't worth it. The deputy glanced down and smiled back at her, putting his hand over hers on his arm.

Now was a good time to remind him this was an act, not reality. While that was never necessary when she worked with other cops undercover, this deputy was all about honesty, so any misunderstanding could go bad.

She leaned closer. "Just a reminder, Deputy, we need to look like a happy couple, not get carried away. Just as an FYI, I don't like being picked up or handled."

"Understood."

They walked a short distance before he spoke again. "Just to be clear, I have no interest in bossing around women. Clearly your past experience with men was about as bad as mine was with women, so let's just leave it at that. I am more than able to control myself and to be a gentleman." He barked out a laugh. "I'm more afraid of you than you probably are of me."

"Fine," they both said at once, then both laughed.

"Maybe we should relax." She winked. "I'll not bite."

He winked back. "I wouldn't mind."

They waved to Noah through the coffee shop window as they passed the bookstore. Danny's response should have given her a bit of relief, but instead Andi found it unsettling. It's not like she thought he was falling for her or anything, she just wanted to ensure clarity so there wasn't a misunderstanding. His response seemed a little uncalled for, but it really didn't matter.

They wandered into the café and ordered some brunch. She nibbled on a muffin while he scarfed a whole dozen-egg omelet. She figured he probably spent his entire paycheck on groceries. A few of the morning joggers stopped to chat and introductions were made all around. No one wanted to talk about Jamie Morrell.

The joggers all exited the café and as the waitress cleared their dishes, Andi sighed. "This didn't seem to be as productive as I'd hoped it would, so far."

Danny looked at her over his coffee. "Don't worry, by tomorrow every single person we talk to will have told ten more and within forty-eight hours we will get some answers."

She chuckled as if he'd said something funny, then leaned over and kissed his cheek for the benefit of those who watched them. Danny's cheek muscle tremored. She allowed herself a little satisfaction. She may not be his type, but he certainly reacted to her touch.

"Why don't we head over to my Jeep and take a drive around? See if we can run into some different people?"

He nodded. "Good idea. A bunch of the older locals spend Saturday fishing the river and they would be good to talk to."

It was a short walk back to the cabin. Andi walked a few paces ahead of him.

She began to relax. Who knew playing girlfriend to an adoring boyfriend could be so nerve-racking? Her kissing his cheek hadn't helped. She'd meant it to be relaxing but it wasn't.

He should have told her to warn him if she was going to do that, not just glare at her in shock. Her surprise had gone against her rules.

As Dan seemed to delve deeper into his thoughts, they hiked toward the lodge and her cabin just beyond.

Minutes later he bumped into Andi, who had come to a dead stop. She was staring at the Jeep still partially hidden by trees. He looked it over, but nothing seemed out of the ordinary. "What?" he said to her.

Andi didn't move.

"What's wrong?" His head was suddenly on a swivel looking for anything or anyone that didn't belong.

She started forward but walked a wide circle around the Jeep, coming up on the side of the vehicle to peek in. He followed, keeping step with her and fully on alert. "The Jeep isn't locked," she said, "and I know it was when I parked it here."

Her steps slowed as they walked near the Jeep and he slowed as well.

"I left it locked with mud on the handle," she said. "I learned that in the wild hills of Mexico. Unless it is raining, I can see the mud on the handle from ten feet away. I'll know someone has messed with my vehicle."

Dan raised an eyebrow. That was smart, very smart. He turned over this fact and what it might mean and scrutinized every detail as they crept closer.

The rental looked undisturbed until they neared the front passenger window. The console papers were askew and scattered on the floorboard as if they had been searched.

"Why would someone search your Jeep?" They started to walk away as if the Jeep was of no interest.

"They weren't looking for anything specific, just wanted me to know they know I'm here."

The large white clouds that had grown in the sky all morning seemed to darken. Danny prided himself on being able to feel trouble coming, but this time he knew, trouble was already here and Andi was being watched.

He wasn't a man who sought out danger if there was any other way, but this time, he was in. When he saw her eyes, he knew she felt the same. If they found her here, then nowhere was safe. The time for running was over; now it was a fight. He kissed her forehead like lovers do. "Stay alert," Dan said against her hair and pulled her into the circle of his arms as he scanned the trees. Nothing out of the ordinary, but he felt eyes on them.

Tugging her hand, Dan steered them toward the lodge and her little cabin. They may know she's here, but the cabin offered more privacy and was easier to defend than open space.

The old man who ran the lodge came out and started to talk

about the weather as he waved them into the lobby that looked more like the three bears' home without Goldilocks.

The minute the door closed, the old man, called Digger, said, "Noticed your Jeep right after dawn when I put out the mail. Passenger's door was not completely closed. Saw footprints circling it, but they've been erased by now."

"See anything else?" Dan asked.

Andi turned her back to the windows and said softly, "I left nothing in the car of interest. Just a few maps and a pack of gum, but they were working fast. At least two."

The old man pinned her with a stare. "They might have been scared off. I had several fishermen come in late." He studied her. "How did you know there were more than one?"

"Both doors were forced open." Andi met the old man's eyes. He was ancient but his stare told her he was aware. He missed little.

"Anything else strange?" Danny kept his sights on the windows.

The lodge owner wiggled his eyebrows as if he knew a secret. "Besides a deputy sleeping outside the last cabin? I should charge you, Deputy Davis."

Danny straightened. "That's official business, Digger. What else did you see?"

"I've seen my share of police business over the years, but all I've heard was snoring lately."

All three stood silent until Danny said, "Anything else going on that I should know about?"

Digger finally stared outside. "I don't know if this is connected, but I smelled gas early, just before dawn. I looked around. If I was a betting man, I'd say your tank has been drained."

"I was low on gas yesterday when I pulled in but not empty."

Both men followed her outside and watched her try to start the rental Jeep. Empty.

Danny took Andi's hand as she stepped out of the car. "Looks like we're walking to supper."

The owner of the lodge headed inside, talking to himself. "Too late for lunch and too early for dinner. Why don't you kids just have coffee or ice cream for a snack? Something funny is going around and I'll bet you it's more police business than private business."

As they walked away Dan said, "Forget ice cream. I don't eat snacks; never have. If I stop to eat, might as well eat a meal."

Andi was barely listening to the rambling deputy. He was lightly moving his hand over her back. She thought of ordering him to stop, but it felt nice.

Ten minutes later they were on the far quarter of the square. She leaned closer and said, "Fill me in on who you are, facts about you that most folks in town would know."

He was silent for a few minutes, as if the question was too hard for him, then finally he spoke. "Graduated from Honey Creek High because it's the only school big enough to have a football team in the valley. I went to college at Texas Tech on a free ride thanks to football. Been a deputy for two years. Before that I was a fireman for almost three years. I took a year off after college and just wandered around. I've lived over by Someday Valley all my life except when I lived in the dorm. My folks have land thirty miles away. It's a drive but I like the work here and the job is never dull. We raise horses, chickens, and hogs, and I help with the farming when needed."

"You live with your parents?"

"Nope. I live in our barn. I like it there. After growing up in a house with six brothers and sisters, I like the silence.

"Some of my sisters and brothers built their houses on our land and some moved to town, but all my kin live in the valley. If you're still my girl, tomorrow, you'll have to have your knees under the Sunday Davis dinner table."

"Didn't you want your own place, farm boy?" she asked as

they neared town. "I had my own apartment in DC at eighteen. My stepfather came by every week. He'd take me out for a meal and ask if I was ready to come back home. When I said no, he'd tell me to study hard, eat right and be in by ten because nothing good happens in DC after dark."

Danny leaned toward her. "Why did you like a tiny little two-room apartment where you can hear the folks upstairs and downstairs? Smell what everyone is cooking and hear every fight anyone for a block has? Sounds from the street wake you all night. I learned during my wandering year that it's best to be alone." Dan grinned. "In the barn all I hear is nature."

For a minute she thought he would say something else, but he stopped. A sadness covered his face and he removed his hand from her back.

He tried to smile but his eyes wore sorrow so deep she didn't want to ask a question.

Finally, he added, "In the barn I hear the horses moving around at night and a rooster is my alarm. I wake up with the sun smiling at me and listen to mockingbirds. I can air-dry just by opening the loft window."

"Too much information," she said trying not to use her imagination. She'd traveled the globe. Spoke three languages. Had fallen in love several times. Usually, her affairs lasted about as long as a cold, and she'd almost died more times than she could count. But she'd never known a man like Danny. He was open and seemed honest to the core. Polite. And funny in his small-town kind of way.

She'd always felt sorry for people who lived in small towns. No nightlife. No theater. No great restaurants. Nothing happening. The world could end and Honey Creek would miss it.

But the strange thing was, no one in town seemed to care.

For one night Andi didn't want to remember that there were a few people who'd like to know what she knew about drug trafficking or have a hint who she's flying from one secret meeting to another. Danny didn't pry. He seemed to accept her as she was.

Andi grinned to herself. "I'm a world of secrets and codes, and a few are all mine."

"Not me. I'm an open book, Andi. I couldn't even remember my locker code in school. Never locked it."

"Didn't you get robbed?" she asked as they headed toward the town square. Andi laced her hand in his.

Dan shook his head. "Only once."

She stopped and faced the deputy. "Don't tell me you beat some kid up over a pencil or a book taken?"

"No," Danny said, "my little sister beat him up for me. By the fourth grade Inez was bigger than any of the sixth-graders. I wasn't much of a fighter in school, but she was. When she was in the sixth grade, she walked over to the high school to beat up a boy in the ninth who yelled at her."

"What happened?" Andi asked. "Did she get expelled? Was he hurt?"

Danny shrugged. "I don't remember how that fight ended. When they were little, they fought on the playground at least once a week. Ten years later they married. You can ask her tomorrow at Sunday dinner."

She tugged him toward the same café where they'd had lunch. She could have sworn the same people were still there.

After sliding into a booth, Danny told her he rarely left Texas. The year he'd wandered, after college, he didn't find another place he wanted to stay more than a few days.

Andi bet he'd never pulled his service weapon. They had nothing in common. He was writing speeding tickets and she was saving others who found themselves in danger.

Before she could tell him that her life was nothing like his, Danny said, "I've had a great life as a lawman. I help people mostly. I like that."

"Me too," she said. "Now and then I help them go to prison."

All Dan answered was, "Me too."

As the sun dropped behind the courthouse, they talked. The shadows of night blended into the shadows of town.

When they walked out of the café, she slid her hand down his arm and laced her fingers in his. The feel of him was growing on her. "You got any idea how we met, Danny? If not at Texas Tech. I'm guessing that's the question they will ask."

"Sure," he said. "I picked you up at the bar in Someday Valley. That's how everyone meets if they hadn't paired in high school or college. I looked at those long legs and realized I could see your pretty face if I danced with you. I decided you were perfect."

He laughed. "Turns out it's hard to talk to the top of some girl's head and dance."

She elbowed him. "That's nothing. Try dancing with a guy with his nose bumping your breasts."

Dan put his arm lightly over her shoulders. "I'll think about which is worse."

She poked him. He tickled her. And, as simple as that they both relaxed. They walked beneath the trees as the cold settled in for the night.

Finally, she said, "That story wouldn't work, Deputy. The people in Someday Valley would wonder how come they'd never noticed me if I grew up around here."

"Right," he agreed. "You're not a girl anyone would overlook. Any chance you were ugly your senior year?"

A quick laughed bubbled from her. "How about I tell people we met online?"

"Fine," he said. "And just for a note, I love the way you laugh."

She didn't comment. He relaxed.

After a few minutes she asked, "You do know how to use a computer, Deputy?"

"Yes. I was into IT in college and I still play around with

cyber security," he shot back. "How about this for how we met? We both went to Tech like I said. You love football so you staked me out."

"Of course. You were my date most weekends that spring of my senior year in college."

Danny added more to the pretend-story as they walked. "I got to second base on our first date. Then after graduation, you moved west and I moved south. After years of chatting online you came down to have another look at me."

She popped her fist into his hard stomach. No reaction. The man was a rock.

He barely moved, then took her fist in his hand, brought it to his lips and kissed her fingers just in case anyone might be watching. "Why'd you do that, honey?" he said calmly. "I have a feeling dating you comes with bruises."

She pressed her lips against his throat and said, "You didn't get to second base in a dating history."

He straightened and kissed her nose. "You're a hard woman to date."

"No kidding. I'd like you to remember I'm armed."

As they passed the bakery, he didn't even glance to see if it was open. "How about I buy you dessert? If the lights are on, they still have sweets to sell. After five, it's takeout only."

"You don't have to buy me anything, Deputy," she snapped as they stepped inside a bakery that was closing up.

Danny raised his voice a bit. "Of course, I'll feed you, honey. You're my girl." He turned to the teenager sweeping. "Got any cookies left, Shirley?"

Andi fell into character as they walked inside. Smiling and patting his arm. They even held hands until the cookies were chosen. They moved close, almost touching. They both were playing a game neither ever played.

Danny seemed relaxed, but this was his valley. He told her about one of his mom's prized chickens while the girl bagged three dozen cookies. "One chicken always watched the house dogs go in and out the dog door. Then the chicken would go to the dog's door and peck on it as if she was knocking to get in."

Andi knew nothing about live chickens. "Won't the dogs eat the chickens?" she asked Dan.

"No. After the dogs get too close to Mom's chickens and she bats the dogs with her broom, the dogs don't even look at the hens."

Andi chuckled and noticed the girl behind the counter did also.

She almost brushed his ear when she asked, "Does it hurt the pups?"

He kissed her cheek. "I don't know about the dogs, but it really hurt me when she bopped me for running after the chickens when I was about five. Mom claimed she didn't want her eggs scrambled before they popped out."

While Andi was laughing, the girl delivered their bags. Then she looked at Andi and winked.

The deputy had eaten all his meal of chicken-fried steak and half of hers at the café. There was no way he could eat three dozen cookies the size of saucers.

On the way back to the cabin, they talked about how he could help with finding her relatives. If her father had passed through the three little towns in the valley, even lived there for short times, there had to be some record besides just the address and electric bill. If he hung out at the local bars, someone might remember him. Andi figured if she found one of Jamie Morrell's sons, he might know where the others would be.

She'd never told anyone but she'd always wished she had siblings. With her father in the Army, he was more like a vacation dad. They'd go see him or sometimes he'd come home for a month, then gone.

Dan broke into her thoughts. "I could ask the old sheriff what he knows. I remember when I came back from the training academy, one of the other deputies mentioned trouble about a will. We'll start there tomorrow," he said as he squeezed her hand. "You know, Andi, I want to say I had a great date tonight. I just wanted you to know before you start threatening to kill me again."

He waited.

All she said was, "Me too. It was fun pretending."

They walked along the bank of the creek. "Danny, the creek really does sound like it's babbling."

"Not much on nature, are you, honey?"

She looked up at him. That was the second time he'd called her a pet name. Alarms went off in her brain. She was getting too close. Follow the rule, *Never get near or you'll cry when they die.*

"Nope. Mud. Bugs. Storms. Nature is either too hot or freezing."

"You cold?" Without waiting for an answer, he opened his jacket and tucked her in against his warmth.

"We put on a great show tonight, didn't we?" She smiled at him. "We make a good team."

"I wasn't acting. It was like we were friends." He placed his hand over her fingers that rested on his arm.

She shook her head. "We're not, Deputy. In a few days I'll be gone and you will never see me again. I don't keep friends, lovers, even family except a card now and then. I just need to know the men who claim to be my brothers are safe, then I'll vanish."

"What about the Texas Ranger I saw you talking to? He matters to you, doesn't he?"

"Once there was more between us, but he insisted I leave my job. I wouldn't and he wouldn't accept less. I'm just someone that he checks on now and then. No more."

"Where is home, Andi?"

"I started as a pilot. It seems above the clouds is more home than anywhere. I guess I'm one of those animals who doesn't need a flock, a pack, or a herd."

He slowed halfway between the town and the cabin. "You've got a few things to look into. Find your half-brothers, make sure they're safe or at least warned. Then we have to look into who messed with your Jeep. That might be nothing, or you do have someone moving in on you."

Dan stood facing her. "Whatever this is in Honey Creek, I'll be beside you."

Chapter 12

Saturday's Confusion

Noah was in his bookshop an hour earlier than usual on Saturday. He started the coffee and made sure all the cups were clean. A few of the walkers drank the coffee and put the empty cups back as they did at home.

He even scrubbed the windows and organized the magazines. Then he tried to think where he and Cora would sit to talk when she came down. Maybe she'd stop to have a cup of coffee. She'd done that before. No one would think anything of it.

After last night on the roof and their kiss in front of her door, he had to see her again. He had to hold her. Touch her. Make plans for what comes next.

He almost laughed out loud. Deep down he wanted to see her to know last night really happened.

He'd never been a dreamer. He had rarely wasted time on fantasies. Those things were not allowed in his house growing up. But just this one time he let his mind fly.

Maybe they could be a couple. She had kissed him full-out. She'd called him *her Noah*.

Maybe they could eat dinner together sometimes. Who knows, he might go to church with her tomorrow? And, maybe, they'd kiss goodnight so often it became a routine.

He stared out the bookstore window. The day was dark and rainy, so Noah could lock up early and he and Cora could start their date. He might suggest driving out of the valley and eating dinner miles away from the people who knew them. A restaurant with candlelight and soft music would be perfect. No drive-thru. No truck stop. No fast food.

For the first time since he left New York he wished he could take his date out to a fancy restaurant. But a cold front moving in made Noah think about just going to the square café tonight. If the wind slowed, he thought of taking her to the roof after eating, or maybe he'd suggest they step into one of their apartments. If they did, they'd be warm and he could see her clearly as they talked.

"My date, my Cora," he said to himself, and shook his head. She wasn't his lady. A few kisses on the roof in the moonlight didn't change anything really.

If he could just kiss her goodnight in the hallway, he'd tell himself that would be enough. He'd worn loneliness so long it felt like a second skin.

It seemed all his life he'd rationed happiness. *Only one piece of dessert. You can check out one book. That's enough for now, Noah.* One ride on the merry-go-round. One try, one taste, one time. It seemed his entire life had been restricted.

Those few minutes they'd shared beneath the moon last night seemed enchanted, another world hidden beneath the ordinary. But she'd said she wanted to see him again, and he wanted more of life for the first time. "More of Cora," he whispered.

In truth, Noah wanted Cora near not for one or two dates but longer, maybe forever. He wanted to hold her hand as they walked and talked about everything and nothing at all.

Usually, his first dates in college ended in a quick kiss, but after a few more study-dates and long coffee meetings, his date would end with her waving and yelling as she jumped from his car, "Had a great time. Thanks. See you around."

He was frequently still standing by the car when he realized the girl had just broken up with him.

Holding Cora Lee eight hours ago seemed more a dream than reality in the daylight. But, it had felt so right.

Noah glanced at the clock, knowing this day was going to drag. He didn't care where they went tonight; he just felt the adrenaline rush in his veins.

The last Saturday of the month Cora would usually run errands for her father. She'd visit her two great-aunts, pick up Bear's groceries for the month, do his laundry.

Noah knew this because next Wednesday Katherine would drill her to make sure all was done.

Cora and Noah were both creatures of habits. They both made lists, but today he didn't want a list. All he wanted to do was think about tonight. What to say? What to do?

Bear once heard him say he wished time would fly by. Bear had frowned and murmured, "Never wish your life away, son."

Noah glanced at the clock again, 8:49 A.M. Time to open the bookstore.

If Cora didn't come down soon, they wouldn't have time to talk. Saturday was usually his busiest day.

He looked at the stairs for the tenth time. No one. No Cora rushing down the steps as if she was tap dancing. Weekdays to school in her plain dresses, Saturdays in jeans to do errands, and Noah usually watched her all dressed up in her Sunday best. If it wasn't raining, she'd walk to church.

Today she'd have on jeans and a sweater. Looking more like a girl than a woman of almost thirty.

He realized he'd measured every day by Cora. For three years he'd watched her rush down. Sometimes she'd smile at him and wave as she reached the bottom where the left glass door turned into the shop and the right door went outside.

The browsers, the talkers, and now and then the readers would soon flood in. All he needed now was time to make plans. How he wanted to kiss her like they did last night. He could still taste her lips.

This morning they needed a few minutes to decide what time they'd leave or where they'd have dinner. He'd already asked for the date last night when he ran back to her room for one last kiss and she'd already said yes. If she hadn't changed her mind, or had something come up, or caught a cold last night, then tonight would be his chance to dive deep into who she was. He wanted to explore all her hopes and dreams and imagine how their lives meshed together.

8:56 A.M. Noah started pacing. Maybe he should go upstairs and make sure she was all right. If she didn't come down now, all she'd have time to say was *Hello* or *See you around*. Which, he'd learned in college, meant goodbye.

One thing that had been on his mind since the wee hours this morning was how she might react when he told her about his plan to be a writer. Would she call him crazy? Would she see him as a loser? Or maybe, just maybe, she'd believe in him and that would make all the difference.

Noah sighed as he looked out his store windows. The first customer was getting out of her thirty-year-old station wagon.

Mrs. Hattie and her half dozen kids marched in, with the mom yelling what they better not do. She thought Noah's bookstore was a playground. Her snotty kids went wild while the always tired mom drank coffee and looked through magazines she'd never buy.

Finally, he saw Cora slowly walking down. Jeans and a sweater. As she reached the bottom, she opened the bookshop door.

Noah's mood was instantly bright, even in the midst of screaming kids. She smiled and walked directly toward him.

There was no time for them to talk, time had run out. People were in the shop.

When she reached him, they both looked at the joggers rushing in, dropping purses, jackets, and water bottles big enough to hydrate a marching band. All eight had thin blue plastic ponchos with BIG BUS stamped on them. Clare Clump went to London a few years ago and brought all her jogging friends one.

Noah didn't even manage a smile for them as his frustration grew.

His new love slipped her hand into his and tugged him behind the first mahogany bookshelf. All the joggers were talking at once without even noticing the teacher and the bookshop owner had disappeared.

Her lips touched his for only a second then she said, "Meet here at six. You pick the place." A smile lingered on her face. "I just want to be with you."

He nodded and she was gone as the bell over the door chimed again. Noah couldn't move as she disappeared. For a moment he could still feel her hand in his.

"That was easy," he said to himself as Mrs. Hattie yelled that she was leaving. Suddenly he was in a race to make sure she didn't forget even one child.

As her offspring lined up, Noah couldn't stop smiling. *I got a date and a kiss*, he thought. *Everything is working out. She didn't say "see you around."*

It was midafternoon before Noah was once again alone with his thoughts. He'd gone over their time together in his mind repeatedly, worrying about the right things to say tonight.

Noah realized that words weren't as important as he thought. They'd said little, but felt much. Still, he wanted to know everything about her. A dozen questions came to mind, but he couldn't think how to ask them without feeling pushy or invasive.

Timothy the mailman rushed in, dropped the mail on the

counter, poured his own coffee in his own mug and murmured something about rain coming in as he walked out.

Noah took a deep breath and said to himself, "I got a lady. I got a date." Saying it made it more real.

He'd thought about what would happen if things went much further than kissing tonight. He had to find a way to let her know he wanted a real love. Not a maybe tonight, or maybe for a week, he wanted a forever.

At five o'clock he locked the door and went up to get ready. The day had turned darker and looked like it might rain the night away. No one would face the storm to buy a book.

He thought about what Cora had meant when she said she wanted it all.

He'd slept with a few girls his freshman year. Right now, he couldn't remember their last names. And the one night he'd shared with them had been more than enough. He never called them and they didn't even bother to wave when they saw him. Six months later he met one at a party and she reintroduced herself.

At one minute until six, he heard rain tap on the window as he sat in the shadows of the bookshop. The lights blinked, then went out.

He tried to think positive. If the slow rain stopped by the time she came down, they'd just walk to the café. He'd carry an umbrella in case the rain started again and the lights might be back on soon.

He heard her walking toward him in shadows. Lightning lit up the sky as if arguing with Noah's idea that they walk. Almost like a primal instinct Noah reached for her and she melted into him. Her hand cupped his face and he smiled into her palm.

When the lightning vanished as fast as it came, he asked, "You frightened?"

She smiled. "I'm a Texas girl. I'm not afraid of nature. How about you, big city man?"

He was silent, then took a deep breath. "If I am afraid, will you stay just a little longer right where you are?"

"Of course. But not long, it's cold down here."

Neither said another word as they watched the lightning show outside start once again. He moved his hand down her back. She wasn't afraid of him but he decided he should step away. Go slow. Remember everything he was supposed to do, everything he'd planned to do to make this perfect.

"Cora," he said. "We don't have to go out. I'm happy right here."

Rain washed past the window in waves. Only a fool would go out if the storm got worse. Noah knew the date was ruined. They'd be soaked if they even tried to run to his car.

"I'm sorry," he said as he kissed her forehead. "I was so looking forward to our date. I wanted to take you to eat somewhere nice so we could really talk. I even thought we might drive over to the Someday Valley Bar. I heard they had a real Nashville band playing tonight."

Quiet Cora suddenly pushed away from him and held out her hand. With the storm rattling the windows, Cora led him, without a word, upstairs using the lightning flash as their only light. The entire town slept in midnight blue.

Once inside her apartment, Cora said, "I have soup I can heat on the gas stove. The burners will give off enough light for us to eat and talk."

"Sounds perfect. While you start, I'll run to my place and get candles. My mother mails candles, Halloween candy and a basket of fruit every fall."

When he got back, the soup was on the stove. Noah spread out seven fat little figures about six inches tall and dressed in red and green.

As he lit their hats, she asked, "Santa's helpers?"

"No, I think they're Snow White's dwarfs that Mom re-gifted."

They settled in with candlelight. As she stirred the can of soup, he moved his hands around her waist and lightly leaned his body against her back. He felt drunk having her so close.

When she pulled away to pour the soup, he felt the loss of her warmth. She didn't meet his eyes. The fragile magic was put on hold.

They drank the soup from mugs and relaxed on the couch. He told her why he moved to Honey Creek and she shared the town's history. She mentioned the Apache legend books that had been burned years ago thanks to a traveling preacher. Some folks tried to save at least one of the books from the fire because the stories held the town's myths that had been told over fireplaces for hundreds of years by the Native Americans.

This night seemed born for telling legends.

She even told him about Holly Rim's dark curses as his writer's mind sparked ideas.

For as long as anyone could remember, people who went near the rim vanished. Some say the woods and rough cliffs swallowed them up. Others claimed someone or something killed them if they got too close to a secret only the Apache knew. Still others said locals found openings in the wall of the rim and they never came back once they passed through, as if it was some kind of portal.

At campfires, kids told stories of a grim reaper who lived among the holly and caught bad little children and drank their blood, then tossed them in one of the caves so deep that not even the smell of rot could climb out.

There was also a rumor that some have seen a native woman who guards the land and lets no one enter. No one investigates the area because they are afraid. The legends protect her.

As the storm raged, Noah lifted a quilt and wrapped them in it. As an hour passed, she settled in beside him as if they'd been together for years. When she rested her head on his shoulder, he kissed her gently. Not a first kiss that held hesitation but a forever kiss that would grow.

Noah decided now was the time to share with her his desire to write. Nervous energy climbed his spine and he cleared his throat and then chickened out a little. Instead, he asked her a question. "Can I ask you how you can be so patient with your sister's rambling complaints?"

Cora was silent for a moment, and he felt a slight smile against his forehead. "Well, it's not what you think. It's not so much that I put up with her, it's that I really feel sorry for her."

Noah was surprised at that. "Why?"

"Kat has spent her whole life chasing happiness. She's chased it with her looks, with husbands, with money, and she still doesn't understand why she can't find it."

Noah turned that over in his mind. He hadn't thought about it from that perspective and it was eye-opening.

Cora continued, "Now, I know that I don't have a perfect life, but I have a very satisfied life. I love to teach, I am glad I get to spend time with my family, even Katherine, and I know I can choose when and how to live. My happiness isn't dependent on anyone or anything because I carry it in here." She touched his chest. "Happiness is never something you find, it's something you create."

They sat in silence for a while as he mustered his courage. Finally he began, "There is something that I've never shared with anyone. Is it okay if I share it with you?"

Cora nodded.

"Ever since I left New York I have tried to write a novel. I haven't made much progress, but I'm committed to making that part of my life." He braced himself and looked away, preparing for what might come. His mother's constant criticism and his father's frequent barbs flooded his mind. It seemed as if time crawled and he slowly turned back to await his fate.

Cora's sparkling eyes meet his and her sweet voice drifted

over his soul. "I think that is a wonderful goal and the perfect career for you. I know you will write a book that will change lives and I can't wait to see it." Her small hand covered his. "How can I help?"

"You can believe."

For the first time, his belief that he could really create this, the life he so desperately wanted, suddenly seemed within reach. Her belief was the safety net he'd always longed for.

He could now say, this felt like home. She felt like home.

He'd finally found home.

Chapter 13

Tell Me a Story

Sunday

Andi sat on the porch of her cabin and enjoyed the slow rain. Everywhere she traveled in the world she liked to watch the storms. A downpour always made the place seem small, as if the walls of the world were closing in.

She'd told Danny she had no home. Even when she was a kid traveling with her stepdad and her mother to military bases and embassies around the world, she'd searched for a place where she belonged.

Her mom told her that for some people home is a person, but Andi didn't believe her. Andi had never had a man she couldn't walk away from. Even when she went back to DC for a holiday, she was ready to fly out within a week.

She watched as Danny marched his way down the muddy trail toward town. Once it got dark, he wanted his pickup parked close in case they had to make a fast getaway.

The sheriff told the deputy that a few strangers had been asking around about a tall woman new to town. Then, before she could argue that it was probably a coincidence, he was walking back to the station. The man reminded her of a Clydesdale horse. Big, powerful.

They'd had nothing but a break-in with her car since she came to town. That could happen anywhere, to anyone. But one thing she'd learned about her deputy was he did his best.

Andi was sure he had cop blood in him. He lived, breathed, and thought like a cop. She'd learned that he wasn't dumb and he moved faster than most men over six feet tall. He was always polite. And he had something else she rarely saw; he was good to the bone. Her stepfather was honorable and caring like that. She'd only known Danny a short time, but she trusted him like she trusted Pop.

Two men in different worlds but cut from the same cloth. Maybe there were hundreds, or millions. She never took the time to look. She was too busy seeing the bad ones.

She stood still for a while, listening to the rain. For once she just wanted to relax and breathe, but the silence ended as the pickup splashed down the dirt road. Danny stopped fifty feet from her cabin, as if he wanted to hide the old truck in the trees.

She smiled, remembering what Danny said yesterday while they were rattling around in the pickup. "No one but a fool would ever sell a running pickup. I'm not sure, but I figure my dad thinks it is the Eleventh Commandment."

The words were pure Texan.

"Look," he yelled as he jumped out of the cab and started splashing through mud puddles toward her. "I brought tacos for breakfast in the morning, and your mail. Sheriff called and said it was addressed to the station. Must be important 'cause it's an overnight delivery."

Danny kept talking as he marched toward her. "Pecos had me pick up a flyer about two missing teenagers from Lubbock. Rangers out of Austin said they want their pictures in every hotel, motel, and lodge in the state. Digger will put it up in the office. Probably runaways . . ."

Danny's eyes finally met her stare and he stopped talking.

She knew without saying a word that he wasn't thinking of teenagers or the lodge manager at that moment.

Andi almost smiled. He had that look all men get now and then. The look that says, *What did I say?* She hadn't said a word but he knew something was wrong.

She met him on the walk and faced him nose to nose. "I don't get mail, *ever*. Even my mother doesn't know what name I use most of the time. No family! No friends! No one ever mails me."

Dan handed her a fat envelope. "It is addressed to Andi Delane, so it must be yours. Few know you are in town and I'm guessing you told even less people you were coming here." He paused. "I figured it was probably from your Texas Ranger. Just sending info." When she didn't move, he added, "Maybe it's court papers or something."

"No. That's not how I work. Thanks to the internet I keep up with headquarters and my folks by cell and now and then email." She held the envelope out as if it smelled rotten.

He took one step toward her as a bullet flew through the rain and splintered a chip of wood off the doorframe between them. One bullet.

Peace shattered. One shot ripped all beauty from nature and seemed to echo like a thunderclap.

Both jumped through the door. Tacos flew to the rafters and fixings splattered down as Dan slammed the door and Andi pulled the weapon from her ankle holster. For a moment they were both trying to get in front of the other. Him to protect her and her to get a clear shot. In the rain it would be a blind shot, but she might get lucky and wing the shooter.

Suddenly the cabin was silent except for the rain tapping on the roof. She could hear Dan breathing. She felt the warmth of him inches away.

In a low breath she ordered, "Lay flat, Dan, and be ready to fire. I'll take point."

"No. I'm here to protect you."

"No way. You're a bigger target."

For a blink he lifted his fist as if planning to knock her down. Then he said firmly, "You need to be low, safer, behind me. It's my job to keep you alive."

There it was again, she thought. The man who had to do what he thought was right.

She touched his arm. A gentle touch. She nodded once. "We do this together." They both lowered their guns and she pointed at the door. "On three we charge," she said as she lifted one finger.

Two fingers. Silently they raised their weapons.

All was quiet outside. Dan slowly opened the door an inch and she watched the windows behind them. Only the trees moved in the breeze as the rain slowed.

Nothing. All around them seemed to hush. Both held their breath.

They waited. Andi's "three" didn't come. They just listened.

The tap of a boot stepping on the far end of the porch almost sounded like a shot. The open door blocked the intruder's view but both knew trouble was near.

A low voice came from the other side of the door. "Come out, Detective. We know who you are. You're surrounded. Thanks to the mail, the deputy brought us right to you. We don't want to kill you. Our boss just needs to chat. If you play along with us, we'll leave the big deputy tied up with a leg wound."

"No chance!" Dan's answer came hard and fast. "I hate seeing my own blood. She is under the protection of the Honey Creek Sheriff's Office. She's going nowhere."

A few of the shadows scoffed, making it easy for Andi to locate the intruders hiding behind the trees. Three, she guessed, or four maybe, besides the leader behind the open door. If they made a move to attack, at least three would be dead before the leader could get one shot fired.

From the corner of her eye Andi watched Dan pull out his cell, push three times and drop the phone back in his pocket as he yelled, "I don't know who you think we are. I'm more than her guard. The lady is my girlfriend. I don't know why you want to talk to her. She is just in town to see me. Anywhere she goes, I go, and she doesn't look like she wants to go anywhere with you guys.

"All we are doing is turning in for a quiet night. And I'm in no mood to be bothered."

Dan was drawing their attention, giving Andi time to search the land.

"Three to the right, two straight ahead," she said.

He nodded once.

The shadow closest to the other side of the door hesitated. Dan didn't give him time to think. He began firing questions. "You are making a big mistake. Did you see her? It's dark. It's raining. If she's not the person you're looking for and you kill me, they'll never stop hunting you. If you drag her to your boss and she's not the woman he wants, you'll be dead."

Andi stared at Dan. He just kept talking.

"I should tell you guys that we're armed. The first head that pokes in the cabin won't have a place to put his hat," Danny said. "What is your boss gonna say when you bring in the wrong woman? He'll probably pop your head off just to free your worthless brain. My boss, the sheriff, hates the paperwork. He'll go nuts if this county has a murder or kidnapping. I saw him put three bullets in a man's leg for shooting the neighbor's dog. Sheriff Pecos made the dog shooter sign a statement saying it was a failed suicide before he'd drive the guy to the clinic. Folks say blood dripped all along the route because Pecos made the dog-shooter hang his leg out the window."

Andi stared at the deputy and decided the man was crazier than the outlaws.

"Let's kill him." Another shadow ID'd himself to Andi as he yelled, "He's lying!"

Danny laughed. "Oh, I forgot to tell you boys another fact. This lady has two brothers. If you hurt their little sister Hell will be better than where they lock you up."

Several voices argued and the leader behind the door began to back off the porch.

Danny yelled as he moved toward the door. "Leave your weapons or the posse surrounding you will shoot if they see even the shadow of a gun."

"What posse?" one silhouette to the left yelled.

No one moved for a moment, then somewhere in the night the rack of a shotgun sounded.

Andi smiled. Dan wasn't bluffing.

A shot filled the night and seemed to echo off the trees.

"Hold your fire, men," Dan ordered. "Give them three seconds. If there is one shot from the trees, open fire." He raised his voice. "This is over. Drop your guns NOW. The only out is the river."

The leader near the door yelled. "Run, men. We're outnumbered."

"You bet your ass you're outnumbered!" a stranger near the back of the cabin yelled.

A shotgun fired, rattling the roof all the way to heaven. "Run for the river, boys, 'cause if you pass us, a dozen trained shots will pick you off before you reach the truck you hid in the weeds."

The men dropped their rifles and ran to the river. Andi saw three sheriffs' light bars flashing as they turned in near the lodge office.

She stepped out of the cabin, her weapon still drawn. She could feel Dan's warmth behind her.

"It's over, honey." The deputy's words brushed her cheek. "You're secure." Then he turned to the black of the trees and yelled, "About time you got here, Digger. All you had to do was walk over when I called in. Pecos had to drive. You're getting old, man."

"Shut up or I'll accidentally shoot you."

Digger walked up with his shotgun over his rounded shoulder. "You're lucky I was listening when the code went through."

"You're always listening, old man."

It took a moment to realize that the posse that saved them

was one old man with the biggest shotgun she'd ever seen. Her ears were still ringing when another round hit the roof.

"Dan!" came the sheriff's voice. "You two OK?"

"Yes, Sheriff, thanks to Digger."

Pecos slapped the old soldier on the back. "Thanks, again."

"Again?" Dan said under his breath to himself.

Pecos turned to his deputy. "We'll round up these rats. Take her somewhere safe. Fast."

Andi holstered her weapon and put both fists on her hips. "I do not need anyone to take care of me. I'm perfectly capable of taking . . ."

Danny lifted her over his shoulder and headed for his pickup in a run.

"Put me down. I'll find . . ."

He didn't slow.

She was so angry she would have shot him if she could have reached a weapon. "Deputy, I am going to kill you. Slow. Painful. No one, I mean no one ever handles me."

"I know, Andi, but at least you'll be alive."

Dan ran toward his pickup with an outraged woman over his shoulder. She was calling him every bad word she could think of.

He couldn't let her go. She was a fighter. If he set her down, she'd run after the men trying to kidnap her.

His job was to protect her even if she'd probably hate him the rest of her life. He wouldn't let her get hurt. He'd stand between her and harm.

Somewhere between the kicks and hits to the head he figured something out. He cared about this woman who was trying to kill him.

He cared about her even after he swore he'd never care again.

If he couldn't stop, Dan decided he'd join her in killing himself.

Chapter 14

Love in Autumn

Sunday

Bear taped a note on his shop before lunch Friday saying he was going to market in Dallas. No one ever asked questions. Apparently, folks assumed there were really mechanic conventions and he just went with it. No one knew this one week was the best of the year for him. He'd learned a long time ago that it's not where you go but who you go with that mattered.

He left by noon, telling everyone he didn't want to be late. No one asked for details.

Ten minutes later he'd turned off West Road and headed up to Holly Rim Farm.

Time stopped. They had their last autumn picnic as they watched the fall leaves change. Bear knew nature was changing them too. His fairy was aging and lately he'd felt time stiffening his bones, but when they were together, they might not be young again but something better, something far sweeter. They were all ages. He saw her young when she laughed and strong as she stood her ground. When he touched her, the beauty hadn't faded. And the love just grew like a huge tree in his heart and every leaf a moment he'd never forget.

The first touch of her breast. A kiss so sweet she cried. They talked all night and made love at dawn. Their first fight that made her cry, and he was so angry he couldn't get out a word. The morning he forgot to kiss her goodbye and he drove back for just one kiss.

There was no memory of realizing they loved one another because both had always held the other in their heart.

As Bear Buchanan did before every change of season, he stayed over a whole weekend at Eliza's farm and helped get the place ready for the upcoming weather. They worked together and slept holding each other until dawn. They were alone in their own world.

Today, like every morning they woke up, he acted as if he was still sleeping as she slipped out of bed. She cooked him breakfast and served it wearing only a blanket. He loved knowing she enjoyed taking care of him, and he'd do anything for her. Only when the mornings grew cold and the sun took its time rising, Bear loved holding her while the world seemed to stop and there was no one but them. They talked and teased each other, then they made love. He thought she was the most beautiful in bright sunshine.

Their bodies were wrinkled now and spotted with scars from life, but he didn't see that. Their love was easily given and returned, which made it priceless.

This fall weekend was his favorite of all. They'd made love the first time in autumn. It was almost as if they were married over many ages. His small fairy was with him. At dawn they'd saddle her two old horses and ride along a worn path that she'd known about for years. At the top, they'd relax and watch the sunrise in all its glory and spread over the land. He'd tell her what he'd told her all those years ago. "You fill my heart."

Every year he'd say the same words when they reached the

rim where the whole world seemed wild. "You think you can find your way home?"

And she'd always answer, "Does it matter?"

"Nope, as long as I'm with you. I'll starve but I'll never leave you."

She smiled. "I know the trail down. I see the gold coins. I always have since I was a kid. They guide me home when I ride near the rim."

"Well, I don't see them so I'll have to stay close to you. I've never seen any coins or heard any legend about them in town. I guess only fairies see those coins, and your ancestors remember the facts."

Bear believed her stories. He'd heard a few Apache tales that one of the Apache elders wrote down. One of Eliza's grandfathers had the stories printed. Years later a preacher said they were "of the devil" and demanded they be burned.

But a few stories remained in Eliza's mind. Bear's fairy knew about the cursed gold coins and the secret passage. She told her stories only to him.

The oldest legend was about a trail the Apache followed to a tiny cave no one knew led out of the valley. When the tribes were warring, they'd ride up to the rim and escape through that passage. Years later a few elders sold the secret path to outlaws who wanted to escape a posse. Maybe that part of her story was true, but the part about the outlaws killing their guides might not be. Some folks said the ghosts of the guides still haunt the rim.

But the story of a foreman of a big ranch and his wife killing each other, or the legend of a bag of dripping coins along the climb, Bear wasn't sure about but he loved listening to her tell it. Eliza would make the husband's words hard and frightening and the wife was always shown as the victim.

What he loved was she believed the story. Her words flowed like frost on the wind.

She always started by shaking her head and saying, "I once

heard a sad, sad story of a man and wife who hated one another. He'd beaten her every day for years. A slap if she didn't move fast enough. Kicked her if she talked back. And now and then he'd whip her until her back bled if she asked a question. When bruises healed, he'd beat her again to make sure that she'd never tell that he was stealing a few gold coins every payday from the rancher who hired him.

"The husband figured the boss would never know; after all, he was a rich man. The husband was sure his wife would never tell on him. After all, the husband thought he controlled her."

Eliza always stopped the story and giggled, then added, "Any man who thinks he is in control of a woman is a fool."

Bear would agree and she'd continue her story.

Over the years the bag of gold coins grew bigger and bigger. Some said he planned to kill his wife, bury her in one of the caves near the rim and say she'd stolen the coins and vanished. But he ran out of time. The boss found out before the foreman could carry out his plan.

The foreman saddled one horse, with the saddlebags of gold strapped to his wife's back. When she climbed on behind him, he figured if the boss caught up to them, he wouldn't shoot with the wife between them.

When they reached the path to the escape tunnel, it was too steep for two to ride.

He knew the boss was about to catch up. He had to lighten the load. It was either the gold or the wife.

When the wife began to cry not to be left, the husband pulled his huge hunting knife.

But this time she decided to fight with a tiny kitchen knife she'd brought along.

He stabbed her and pushed her off the horse as he grabbed the bag of gold coins from her back.

As she tumbled, she swung her little blade and wished him dead. Her knife poked a hole in the bag of gold big enough for one coin to pass through at a time.

Riders found her dead halfway up to the rim. The husband made it to the top, but he couldn't find the passage in the dark. When the posse found his horse and the husband dead from a fall on the rocky mountainside, the bag was still in his hands but only two coins remained inside.

Some folks who've climbed near the rim swear they can hear the husband screaming for his wife to come save him.

A dozen men went hunting for the gold the next spring. Eight came back. For years when men rode near the paths, some swore they heard a horse running but no gold was found.

Everyone who knew the dead couple also knew they hated each other so completely they probably followed each other into hell. Some say the Devil took the gold for having to put up with them.

The story was written in the book of legends and then lost after the books were burned. And as sometimes stories do, they shift and bend in the retelling.

Bear had heard Eliza tell the story a dozen times. She always ended with, "Now and then a hiker gets lost in the hills. Some say they see a blink of gold in the dirt guiding them. When they walk toward it, the gold disappears a moment before the hiker sees a way out."

Bear loved listening to her as they lay next to each other. A few weekends a year they were the only two people in the world.

Sometimes he'd surprise her with a visit in the middle of the week when the ache was too much. Or he'd bring dinner and they'd just talk.

No one was aware of their love, but if she died first, he'd never smile again.

If she left him, she'd take his heart with her.

In the morning before the sun rose, he whispered, "Marry me."

And she answered, "I can't. We can't change paradise."

Then he made love to her again, like it might be the last.

Chapter 15

Reality Slams as Thunder Rolls

As the Sunday sky darkened, so did Noah's hopes. The rain threatened again, first pinging against the windows and then coming off the roof like tiny waterfalls. Sunday walkers disappeared off the town square. The lights came on in the café and the streetlights looked like fuzzy balls. His dream of finally having that great date with Cora vanished.

Noah smiled. The "washed out date" last night hadn't turned out so bad. He laughed to himself. Cora Lee Buchanan had a body made for cuddling.

He could almost hear his mother telling him to not get his hopes up for another date holding Cora. Women want to go out on the town. Staying in a little apartment couldn't be fun. But it was for Noah, and he guessed Cora felt the same.

The thought of his mother lecturing him about cuddling ruined his daydream.

You'd think he'd learn. Every time he hoped for something, it always was a disappointment. Christmas growing up was less than he dreamed. Vacations were boring. Even the one time they went camping, it rained and they slept in the car.

If his mother knew he'd spent thirty minutes thinking of Cora's full breast pressing against his side, she'd probably knock him into hell. His parents never mentioned anything about sex or reproduction. He'd spent hours wondering how he had been conceived. He was a test tube baby—the only answer.

Noah didn't want to think about maybe trying a do-over date. But it would be worse when it didn't happen. He told himself he was settled, content with his life. Last night, holding Cora was just nice, nothing more. Neither had mentioned more.

Bear had dropped in Friday to tell Noah he was locking up and heading out. Noah thought of telling his landlord to have fun, but how much fun can a parts convention be?

At five Noah ran up the stairs and changed his shirt and grabbed his jacket just in case Cora wanted to try their dinner date again. He'd already concluded that Cora would call off the date. Any sane person would. They were two shy people. The whole town would talk if they went out. Gossip.

But he'd be ready just in case and if people talked, let them.

He decided if she didn't show up, he'd walk through the rain and eat at the men's round table by the door with the truckers, widowers, and bewildered husbands who'd been kicked out.

He relaxed in the only comfortable chair in the shop, as he did every Sunday. He'd immersed himself in a book. He could have read upstairs in his apartment but he liked glancing outside on the town square while waiting.

He saw Cora fly down the stairs from her apartment, dressed in her Sunday best, at exactly six o'clock. Noah realized she was as excited for their do-over date as he was. Even though they were both adults, he had a hint that she hadn't had any more dates than he had.

"I'm ready, that is if you want to try our dinner date again." She went up and down on her heels.

Noah grinned. She was as enthusiastic as he was about their

adventure . . . He hoped it wasn't the last. Before he lost his courage he straightened and asked, "Would you mind if I kissed you before we leave? I've been thinking about how you taste since we met on the roof, and last night we talked and shared a blanket but we both fell asleep. I'm afraid I'll screw up and miss out on another real kiss."

Cora giggled as if she was still in her teens. "That seems like a great idea. When my hair dries into wild curls, I might frighten you. I didn't want to take the time to dry it. I thought you might not wait for me. You might not want to be too close when it turns into a tumbleweed curl."

Noah just stood in front of her. He hadn't thought much beyond the asking. In a little town there were only a few places to eat and most of the people in any café would know them and stop to talk. If he didn't kiss her first, who knows what might happen.

She seemed to understand. She took his hand and tugged him between the shelves. The bookshop was closed but shy Cora seemed to need privacy. No one would stand in the downpour to look inside the bookshop, but she wanted to be alone with him. Somehow that made it more intimate.

The shadows of the stacks relaxed him. He gently placed his hands on her shoulders and pulled her closer. "I don't know where to take you. If this rain turns to snow, the roads might be bad if we left town." He moved so close their bodies were almost touching. "I just want to be alone with you."

He couldn't say another word as she closed the inch between them and they were pressing against each other as they breathed. "Close your eyes, Cora. I want to kiss you, a keepsake kiss that we'll never forget."

He made his kiss light, but she didn't close her eyes. For a moment she wasn't even kissing him, she was letting him kiss her. When she opened her lips, all thought stopped and both just felt.

Then something happened to shy Cora Lee Buchanan. She

took one step into life and that one step was toward him. She kissed him back and followed him into a need he'd never known to long for.

"Tell me what you want," he said when he finally broke the kiss. He moved his hand down her back. "You've already given me the best kiss ever."

"I want it all, Noah, if only for a night. I've watched you for years. You're a good man, a kind man. For once I'd like to feel alive."

As the bookshop grew darker, he leaned her against the shelves and their kisses turned deeper.

When their heads bumped, they laughed and relaxed a little. When his hand brushed over her breast, she made a sound of surprise.

He stepped back. "I'm sorry. I'm moving too fast. It was an accident."

"Noah, you don't have to apologize. We're not teenagers. I want this as much as you apparently do." She looked around. "But, it's dark and cold here, maybe we should start our date."

"One more, dear," he murmured against her ear as his hand spread lightly over her breast.

As she leaned into his touch, she said, "Mr. O'Brien, I had no idea you were so wild."

"Me either."

Twenty minutes later he finally ended the second kiss. "That was perfect."

"I agree. Where did you learn to kiss like that? I don't think you read it in a book."

He stared at her red cheeks and sparkling eyes. "From you. Just now. You move closer when I get it right and you make a tiny sound when I get it just right. I feel like I'm holding a priceless instrument." His hand brushed lightly along her cheek. "I want to give you what you like and you make it easy."

He brushed his thumb over her lips, then stilled. His kiss was featherlight and tender.

Both waited. Then, she said softly, "Perfect. Would you do it again?"

"Let's go eat. I'm starving."

"For me or food?"

"Both. Eat, run back here so we can be alone."

"We'll find food somewhere and continue this conversation, but first you'll need to remove your hand from my breast."

"Later?"

She smiled. "Later."

He slowly brushed away any fingerprints on her sweater. He hadn't touched her bare skin or even seen her breast, but he felt very wicked and couldn't wait to do it again.

Both forgot to move. He kissed her again. Light kisses while she spread her hand across his chest. Deep kisses as he pressed her against the shelves.

Finally, he pulled away and studied her face. "I think I'm in love with you, Cora Lee."

"Have you ever been in love, Noah?"

"I thought I was, but she broke up with me on a group chat."

He could hear Cora fighting not to laugh, which made him laugh too.

Chapter 16

Plotting Murder

Sunday

The always bossy deputy ushered Andi into the driver's side of the pickup. She scrambled toward the passenger door and planned to escape, but Digger, smelling of fish, bounced into the passenger side of the truck's bench seat. The butt of his shotgun made Andi jump back toward Danny.

Digger yelled, "Floor it, son. I'm riding shotgun on this run."

"What about your guests at the lodge?" Danny hollered as if they weren't right next to him.

Digger hugged his shotgun as the deputy flew down the dirt road by the river. The old man yelled, "Nobody here. Fishing ain't no fun in the rain. Why'd you tell those outlaws to run for the river? It's almost overflowing its banks and cold as a polar bear's butt."

The deputy smiled. "They will jump in thinking they'll escape, but the water is freezing and rough tonight. They'll be jumping out at the first bend. All the sheriff will have to do is pick them up downstream."

Andi finally managed to get a word in. "Drop me at my car."

She figured with a full gas can stashed under Digger's porch and four bullets in her 1911 she could take care of herself.

Danny didn't slow as he flew past the lodge and her car. "The sheriff told me to take you somewhere safe. You're going home with me."

"What?" Andi squeaked.

Before he could explain, Digger jumped in. "I'm going along, too. This little lady needs help. I'll stay on guard."

Andi didn't remind Digger that she was taller than he was, probably a better shot, and trained in several martial arts. All of which she planned to use on Danny as soon as she got the chance.

"You figure your mom got some of that double chocolate cake?" Digger yelled over the engine. "Guarding a lady makes a man hungry."

Dan didn't slow as he made the curves at full speed and Digger, and his shotgun, ended up almost in Andi's lap. Before she could scream, he turned on a two-lane marked CR 45 and just kept talking. "Mom made one yesterday. I guess there are a few pieces . . ."

"Will you two stop talking about food?" Her words bounced around the cab. "We need to figure out who is shooting at us. I've got more than one guy who probably wants to talk to me while he's torturing me."

Digger raised his hand as if they were in a classroom. "There ain't no one shooting at us, miss. I think they are shooting at you. Ain't nobody been shooting at me since 'Nam. I remember nights when the sky lit up like the Fourth of July. There was one time . . ."

"Can we stay on point?" Andi said fairly calmly.

Digger didn't give up. "Oh, we got time for a few stories about my war years. Danny's family farm is the last one down 45." Digger closed his eyes and began, "I was just a boy when I was drafted in '66 . . ."

The deputy leaned close to Andi and said in a low voice, "Who do you think it was trying to kill you, honey?"

"Drop the 'honey' game we've been playing," she said sharply.

Dan nodded. "Oh shucks, I was just getting used to our relationship. How about we talk about it when men aren't chasing us?"

"Not us! Me, remember. I can think of a few drug lords south of the border and one mobster operating in Dallas, then there is a really mean suspect I can ID. Without me, the law can't prove he was at the scene of a crime, so he might be hoping that I die before next week."

"Wow, lady," Digger said more to himself than Andi. "I was thinking that maybe you had a mad ex-boyfriend. I figured he collected a few drunk friends and came to get you back from some handsome Romeo in the sticks. Then during the 'get her back' raid, one of the drunks got off a shot."

Danny swore. "I'm not a Romeo and I know I'm not handsome and this isn't the sticks."

"This could be about her work." Digger jumped into reason two. "From what I've seen, women always have fights going at work. More women, more fights. I bet Andi is one of those workaholics. They need to just talk it out."

Andi looked at Danny. "Can we eject him? His logic is wrong on so many levels."

"No!" Danny said. "He just saved us, remember. The least I can do is feed him cake. If he hadn't come over, there would be blood on the cabin porch and there is a good chance it would have been ours."

Andi twisted to face him. "All right, but can I gag him?"

The deputy patted her leg touching his. "Settle down."

"I'll kill you next," she said. "You are blowing up the danger we were in. Maybe they were shooting just to keep me from testifying."

Digger butted in, "I ain't no idiot, Andi. You're in danger. Why else would Danny be guarding you?"

"Does Andi look like she can't handle an old boyfriend?" Dan asked as if it mattered.

Digger snorted. "I'm surprised any old lovers of Andi's are still alive. If the loving doesn't give him a heart attack, the goodbye fight probably will.

"Wait a minute, you're the new boyfriend, son." Digger's old finger pointed right at the deputy. "Everyone is talking about you two. Taking bets that you'll be married by Christmas. After tonight they'll have another pot going to see if you're alive by New Year's."

"I'm not that easy to kill and I am not letting anyone shoot Andi." Danny patted her leg again as if making a promise.

Andi didn't want to talk to the two idiots she was riding with. She might not know exactly who was after her, but she did know that she was in danger and so were the two men beside her. She had to vanish. Whoever was tracking would keep at it and these two wouldn't be safe. This valley was too little to hide out in.

Dan turned under a gate twenty feet high. "We're home. Three more miles to the headquarters."

"Three more miles? You have to be kidding." All she could see ahead of them was empty pastureland. No houses, no buildings, nothing. It already felt like it had been miles since they'd passed the last farm. This might be secluded enough to work, maybe. At least for the night. Not even a rabbit could sneak up on a headquarters that far from a paved road.

Dan gunned the old pickup's engine. He was finally on his land. She was safe. He could breathe.

Digger kept running on like a book-on-tape. He was reliving another adventure. He remembered every moment during the war. He'd almost died a few times overseas but he was a hundred percent alive when bullets flew.

"Are you angry?" Danny asked Andi.

"Just frustrated."

"I get that."

Dan smiled as he watched the fire light up those eyes of hers. He saw anger and fight in them but he thought he also saw a hunger. She was sitting so close they were touching from knee to shoulder.

"I have to watch over you even if I have to fight you to do my job."

She thought for a few minutes, then she slowly hugged his arm as she had once before. "I get that."

He couldn't find an answer. Not with one of her breasts pressing his arm. And that was as much of a truce as he'd get tonight.

Dan leaned and kissed her head. To his surprise, she didn't flare up again but she didn't look at him.

Digger ended the moment they might have had by yelling, "Are you two listening? I was just getting to the exciting part. We were knee-deep in mud in 'Nam. I had two bullets left and the radio was dead."

The old man kept talking but no one in the cab was listening.

Chapter 17

A Peaceful Chaos

Andi had no idea what Danny's family farm would look like. Somewhere between *Little House on the Prairie* and *Heartland*. Probably a nice house where six kids could grow up and a barn or two for animals. Horses, cattle, chickens, pigs, things like that.

Her mind kept naming critters as the deputy drove. Rats, snakes, fire ants, huge spiders, wild boars, and who knows what else. Suddenly the guys in the trees at Digger's cabin didn't seem so bad. But spiders and snakes didn't carry guns. The ranches of drug lords in South America were more like forts than farms or ranches. Pop took her to see live volcanos when she was a kid. She'd ridden the rapids and swum in every ocean. She'd climbed rock walls at twelve and mapped caves that would have been completely black without flashlights, but Pop seemed to have left out farms and ranches from her education.

That was not what she saw when they pulled into the Davis headquarters. It was more like a small town. "You're rich?" she asked.

"Nope," he answered low. "In good years we build. In bad

years we survive and the bank carries us. Farmers are always one storm away from trouble."

Digger was halfway to the big white house's back door by the time the pickup stopped rattling.

Danny jumped out, held the pickup door and offered her a hand. "You want to walk, or I could carry you over my shoulder?"

"Don't ever do that again."

She climbed out but she didn't take the hand he offered.

He chuckled as they followed Digger. "If I ever do anything you do like, let me know."

One step inside the back door, Danny knelt on one knee. "Give me your boots."

She thought of a dozen reasons why she should refuse that request. She couldn't run without shoes. Farmers never tracked dirt in the house. Maybe everybody takes off their shoes like they do in some countries.

Then she saw the rubber rug. Dirty boots lined up just inside the house. The first room was a mudroom.

It felt strange as he pulled one boot off, then the other. It was something practical to keep the house clean, but also somehow sexy. His hand holding her calf firmly. She touched his shoulder for balance. His sunshine-red curls brushed her hand. For a moment when he looked up, it seemed she could read his thoughts. Danny must have thought the simple gesture was suddenly alluring as hell because he winked at her.

Andi smiled knowing they were thinking the same thing.

All at once she heard screams. She reached for a weapon. Before she could locate one, three preschoolers attacked Dan. He tried to get his boots off as they climbed over him, showing no mercy.

One yelled, "We're coyotes, Uncle Danny, and you are supper."

Dan had one under his arm as he held the other two off. "Well, boys, I'm not dinner."

The second wild creature went under the same arm while Andi just watched. The deputy grabbed the third kid's leg and carried him upside-down.

Number two wiggled free and started fighting his uncle's leg like it was a punching bag.

Dan picked up the escaping boy by the back of his belt and moved toward the big yellow kitchen with open windows letting in fresh air.

The boys' shouts, complaints, and giggles were just background noise to Danny's question. "Mom, when are these coyotes going to be old enough to go to school?"

A lady in her fifties was putting platters of food on a long table. "They start kindergarten next September." Her hair was red with a brush of white and her cheeks were kissed by sunshine. She turned to Andi and smiled. "And you must be Andi. The lady my son is watching over."

Dan was sitting the coyotes in their chairs and tying them in with apron strings. Then he turned to the kind woman who managed to look proper in jeans and a plaid shirt and said, "Mom, I'd like you to meet Andi. We had a little trouble and thought she'd be safer here. You got room for a few more at the table?"

"Always," she said as she moved about the kitchen.

The lady smiled at Andi and frowned at Digger as if Dan let in flies. "The bedrooms upstairs are full but we'll make room."

Dan grinned. "Digger just came along for the ride. Feed him. He saved us tonight." The look he gave his mother silently said *details later.*

She nodded in understanding. "Your father is on the water downstream, fishing with the sheriff. He said to tell you they caught three."

He nodded once, letting his mother know he understood her code.

Dan's mother welcomed her as if she was a neighbor who just dropped by.

Andi watched as a woman looking nine months pregnant waddled in. She said hello to Andi, kissed all three boys, smiled at Dan and ignored Digger.

Dan pulled his sister Summer's chair out and did the same for Andi. She thought of telling him that wasn't necessary, but she had a feeling it was, in this house. He patted Andi's shoulder as if he knew she was feeling a little awkward with all this family. Dan stood until he pulled a chair for his mother. The tablecloth might be faded and everything was in the room to be useful, but the manners were woven into everyday life.

The deputy sat between his sister and Andi, and let his leg brush Andi's. She didn't move again. In a strange way she was growing used to his touch. There was no flirting, no advances, just a solid touch as if to remind her she was safe, protected.

By the time a few other siblings came in, introduced themselves and sat down, the table was full. Food and conversation flowed freely. Some talk was about the business, but mostly just family things. The grown brothers told stories about each other and the little ones played a game kicking one another under the table. Apparently, who yelled out first lost. At least Andi thought that was the game. When she was growing up they were usually just a family of two, or three, if her father made it home. Dinner was always eaten in front of the news and none of her family kicked.

A tall man came in as everyone else was finishing dinner. The older version of Danny kissed the cook. He looked at his son next to Andi and nodded. Introducing himself as Rod Davis, Danny's father had hair as white as snow. He made no comment about fishing but did welcome all the guests.

After the meal, everyone helped clean up while Rod Davis ate, and then the couples paired up. Danny's parents went out to the front porch to watch the sunset. Summer and her husband were living upstairs with their triplets until the baby came. They disappeared to give baths and get the little coyotes to bed. Digger ate the last piece of cake off the serving plate while saying he thought he'd sleep over at the bunkhouse since there was always an empty bunk or two.

Danny's mom smiled at the old man. "I keep your bunk made up. Thanks for helping the kids." She pointed at Digger. "If you get up before seven, eat with the cowhands or sleep in and eat over here at eight."

"Any chance I can make both?"

Everyone laughed and Danny's mom smiled.

Dan's cell rang. He straightened as he answered, then stepped outside.

Andi followed. In the still night she could hear both ends of the conversation.

"You got her somewhere safe?"

"I did."

"Good. I finally found two of her brothers." The sheriff's voice came out clear in the night. "They were fishing and out of cell range the last few days. They said they'd be in by mid-morning. Rusty said he'd meet her but he's got questions and she'd better have proof. He said he wouldn't tell Zach. The kid has had enough letdowns in his life."

Dan answered, "I understand. I'll keep her safe tonight. It's been a long day. No telling what might happen tomorrow."

"You need me to send backup?"

"Nope. I've got Digger to keep watch over her while I check the gates. I'll give him a sleeping bag and put him in the side doorway of the barn where she'll be. He can be on lookout until midnight. Anyone who wants to hurt my charge will have to climb over Digger and get past me."

Andi backed into the shadows as the sheriff told Danny where they'd meet tomorrow. She didn't care what they said; she'd be gone long before daylight. She made a habit of running when trouble grew close. Now that trouble had found her, she'd be smart to put off meeting her brothers.

Surprisingly she felt an ache in her chest. *Brothers*, she almost said aloud.

Just as Danny finished the call, she disappeared into the kitchen once again.

Dan's mom made sure that Andi had everything she needed for the night. A toothbrush, a cotton gown, socks, and a shotgun. She walked Andi over to the barn that Dan occupied when he came home to Honey Creek, while he settled Digger downstairs with the horses. If anyone opened the barn side door, they'd trip over the old guy. If the big barn door swung open it would wake anyone in the place, including all the horses.

Before Andi could climb the rough steps to Dan's barn bedroom, Summer, Dan's very pregnant sister, popped by to tell Andi that Danny and her husband were checking the ranch gates.

Digger was already snoring downstairs. Summer said the horses were complaining about the noise.

As Dan's sister opened the side door, Andi realized she was safe for the night. She could take a shower. She wouldn't be bothered. Danny would be on the landing soon, half a stairway away.

"See you at breakfast," the deputy's sister added. "I know this is his job but I think you are the first girl he's brought home."

Summer was gone with a wave. Andi stepped on the loft floor and looked around at a space that looked more like an apartment than a barn. It appeared she wouldn't be running tonight. She had no worry about locked gates, but she wanted to see her brothers even if just for a moment. Reason told her to run and disappear, but her longing for a family told her to stay.

When she was little, she used to dream of having brothers. In her mind she'd have adventures with them. Rusty must be the oldest. Zach was still a boy.

Perfect names, she thought.

She walked around Danny's place as she murmured her brothers' names.

A big desk was covered with manuals and two computers. It reminded her of the tech room at the Dallas Police Department. Books were stacked around the desk like a moat.

Over by the huge window was a king-size bed. Another huge window on the side of the loft opened out, and she could see the moon shining bright. Five feet of cabinets served as a kitchen on one side, and a bathroom on the other side along with what had to be a closet without a door.

The place seemed to be in organized chaos, designed for a big man, but this was not his home. No pictures. No plants or memorabilia. She opened the refrigerator. Bottled water, butter, ketchup, and various containers of what she assumed to be his mother's great food.

In the open spaces around his apartment were boxes. Some had his name on them; some had other names. One read OLD TOYS. Another PUZZLES. Several were labeled BOOKS.

Her deputy didn't live here; he was part of the storage. He wasn't living . . . he was waiting, almost as if in limbo . . . but why?

Her sharp brain began to put together the pieces of the deputy she'd collected so far:

A month's stack of mail he hadn't read. Not interested.

A dozen novels by his bed. He couldn't sleep.

A whiskey glass full of rattlesnake tails on a shelf of Western novels. He hated rattlesnakes.

A pocket-sized picture of a girl about twenty, worn and nailed to the inside of a cabinet.

Andi moved closer. The picture was so faded it seemed taken in shadow. Curled on the corners and at eye level so he could look at it every time he passed by. Not framed. Not cherished. This picture must only be a reminder.

She guessed. A lost love? A dream he'd once had?

Half a dozen books were open and left half read. It seemed the deputy never finished anything here. What was he waiting on?

Andi guessed something stopped him from leaving the nest, or he came back here on purpose. The saying she'd thought of earlier came back again. *Sometimes home isn't a place. It's a person.* Maybe he lost that person, and he ran back to the nest.

From the looks of it, the deputy hadn't found his place in the world. He'd been a football player, a firefighter, and now something brought him home.

A single tear drifted down her cheek. They were a strange pair, she thought. He couldn't find his place and she'd never had a place where she belonged.

"Are you settling in okay?"

She swiped at her eyes as Danny's voice cut through the silence.

"I'm fine." She gestured at the scattered mess of his room, hoping to distract him. "Are you moving in or moving out?"

Dan barked out a laugh. "Come on, let's go for a ride. I'll show you. I've got to double check the locks anyway."

Once they were in the pickup, neither one said a word. After a few miles, Andi made out the frame of a three-story house sitting next to a spring. A widow's walk wrapped around the top floor, and she imagined the owner would be able to see in every direction. No one would ever surprise Danny in this house.

Dan stopped the truck and said softly, "Someday I'll be moving out here. This is the beginning of my goal."

He stepped out of the pickup and offered Andi his hand. Two steps later they were running toward the someday house.

As they moved through the rooms, Danny didn't let go of her hand, and for the first time excitement shone in his eyes. He smiled, showing her every room in the layout of the house.

She could almost see the end product in all the wood and concrete. They moved through the rooms and she could imagine the home. The living room, the patio, the bedrooms. A huge fireplace, handmade with river rocks that had been placed with care. Oversized windows in every room.

As they walked through the frames of doorways, Andi noticed they were all seven feet tall. In the kitchen and bathroom, the sinks were waist high on her. She could see herself in the mirrors that usually cut the top of her head off. And as she moved through Danny's space she could see that this was a home made for tall people.

"There are so many rooms in this house." Andi laughed.

"Yea, I'm planning for a bunch of little Davises running around."

Andi wondered what a big family would be like. Kids running up and down the stairs. Laughter everywhere.

"I can almost feel the love and laughter that'll be here," she whispered.

As they moved upward, to the third floor, she saw the master bedroom. It was one room, a large bathroom to the side and a shower tall enough to fit her. She stopped in front of a huge window as large as the one in Danny's barn.

Her deputy stepped up behind her and gently put his hand around her waist. "I wanted to feel like I was a part of nature, to be able to see the land from all sides."

Andi stared out into the night. The moon shone high in the sky and she saw the stream beside the house and oak trees that would grow with the family over the years.

She searched for any sign of civilization. "I've lost my sense of direction. Where is this on your land? Is it in the center or on the far west side? Where is it?"

When she was a little girl and traveling the world with her father, he'd taught her to find her markers so she would always know where she was. And right now she couldn't see anything. All she knew was that Danny was with her, and it felt right.

Dan stepped closer and moved his hand up her back. He slowly ran one hand over her shoulders and said, "If your back was a map, this would be north." His hand trailed slowly down to her waist. "This would be south." His fingers brushed along her side. "East," he whispered. His palm moved back across the other side. "West."

He moved his hand gently, stopping in the center of her back. "This is where my home is. In the center. My home is in the middle of the ranch so I can see the dawn and the sunset for the rest of my life."

She shivered. Her whole body seemed cold except where his hand rested gently.

He stepped away and Andi almost yelled out in protest. But a second later he wrapped her in the flannel shirt he'd been wearing and pulled her into him. The warmth of his body heat welcomed her. He leaned forward and she felt his words against her ear.

"Are you warmer now?"

She turned in the circle of his arms so she could see his face. They'd been in gun fights, five-year-old coyote fights, and they'd run for their lives. And not once had her deputy made a move on her. It was about time she took matters into her own hands.

Slowly she pressed her lips to his, barely touching him. He seemed to turn to stone. He didn't object but he wasn't participating. She decided she'd better try again. Full on assault.

She kissed him full out. Danny didn't defend himself. He surrendered. His arms tightened around her as he lifted her off the ground.

For the first time in Danny's life he was in the center of his family's land and he had no idea where he was. It took his whole brain to find his bearings as Andi pulled away. Every cell in his body wanted to pull her back. He saw a different kind of fire in her eyes, one he never wanted to lose. In that instant he knew he was addicted to that glow. He wanted more. He needed more.

He just stared at her. Neither one of them seemed to be able to say anything. Finally he whispered, "Let me show you one last room."

Danny grabbed her hand as easily as if they'd been lovers for years. He took her to the last room in the house. This one room looked like an office space without windows.

"What's this?" Andi asked.

"I can't tell you much about what I really do. I have another job that only the Texas Rangers know about. I'm not just a deputy. They call me the Wizard, and I search for the bad guys on the internet."

His honest eyes focused on her. "I can't tell you everything."

Andi smiled and said, "Let's save this conversation for when we're naked. Right now we've got a lot on our plates."

Danny grinned. "You mean there's a future between us?"

She didn't say a word, but he saw the fire in her eyes and knew there would be.

Chapter 18

Reality Dawns

Monday

Noah wasn't sure he closed his eyes as Cora Lee Buchanan slept in his arms in her apartment above his bookshop, and he didn't care. He held Cora against him as they listened to the rain. They were cocooned in her grandmother's quilt, but unlike last night they were kissing and touching. Now and then they rested and told each other childhood stories they'd never told anyone.

Noah felt half drunk on coffee. Every time he pulled her close and the talking stopped, they went deeper into passion. During relaxing they shared their dreams and fears.

She'd got up twice. Once to lock the door and once to see if it was still storming. When she came back, he smelled mint toothpaste. So, before she could cuddle next to him, he vanished to her bathroom and had a short debate whether to use her toothbrush or his finger.

The toothbrush won out.

He thought of suggesting they sleep together before dawn,

then part before the world found them, but he wanted the loving to come slowly so he'd remember it all. The beginning was so sweet he didn't hurry anything.

It took an hour to kiss her just right, then he moved her hair back and kissed her neck for a while, loving the way she tasted and smelled. Even in sleep she made little sounds of pleasure. He didn't take off any of their clothes but he learned the lines of her body with a light touch.

He kissed her tenderly as he held her against him. She might be sleeping but her body responded to each kiss, every touch. When he finally pulled away, he saw her eyes were open. "You all right, my Cora?"

"Yes," she answered in a sleepy voice. "Don't stop. I feel like I'm dreaming but my eyes are wide open."

His hand moved down her back, bolder than before. His fingers moved, featherlight over her hips. "I'll kiss you until you tell me to stop."

"That will be a long while." She blushed. "I want more, please."

His lips moved over her face as he followed her order. When he finally broke so she could breathe, he said, "If you don't mind, I'd like to touch you . . . and kiss you . . . and taste you while you sleep. I'm suddenly addicted to you." His hand moved over her hip once more and patted her lightly. He wished her jeans were missing, but she deepened the kiss as he patted her again.

They were learning to communicate without words.

"Suddenly you are my world, and somehow, in a blink, I know I'll never be whole without you," he said. "I'll treasure you until my last breath, Cora."

She smiled and wiggled closer. Her lips were swollen and open as he tasted them while his hand rested over her breast once more. "I'm hungry for one more full-out kiss before I let you sleep. Any objection?"

She opened her mouth in answer.

He kissed her like he'd never kissed a woman, as he rolled on top of her. He felt her moving beneath him, settling in, making little cries of pleasure as he learned her body. When she broke the kiss, she turned away but exposed her throat.

"More?" he whispered against her ear.

"Yes," she answered.

His mouth moved down her neck and picked the next place to kiss. Then, as fast as the storm had raged inside of him, it calmed. He rolled on his back, pulling her atop him. She was with him and he realized he couldn't let her go.

Noah pressed light kisses across her face and over her neck. He gently pushed her hair back. He could feel her rapid breathing but he needed to see her face.

"You all right, dear?"

Her words came slow and hoarse. "I've never been kissed like that."

"I feel like I stepped into heaven with you, Cora."

Those big green eyes looked at him with wonder. "What does it mean?"

He studied her as his logical brain returned. "We could go through months talking, even years of moving slow, but I'm thinking it means you're mine. I want you as my girlfriend, my partner, my mate. I want you by my side. I want you next to me every day and night. I feel like a caveman showing up at your cave. I don't know what to say, but you are mine and, whether you want me or not, I'm yours."

Noah frowned for a moment. He was either the worst lover or he was speaking from his heart. He always thought love grew over time, but loving Cora seemed to hit him in the head like a lightning bolt.

She wiggled a few inches away. "I know we're not kids, but is this too fast? Shouldn't we think about what we're running into?"

Noah, always a logical man, figured his brain had died and his heart had taken over.

He tried to let reason rule. "We could date for a year. You could meet my parents. We could plan a wedding. We could date other people." As he made his list, he could sense Cora's *see you later* breakup speech waiting in the corners of his brain.

Only he had never felt so alive. If she ever said those three words to him, he'd crumble.

While he stared at her he pulled another list into his thoughts. All the things he did wrong. Moved too fast. He should have told her how pretty she was, how smart, she was kind. He'd been watching her for three years.

And worst of all, he hadn't treated her like a lady. Cora was a gentle soul. He should have taken her to a fancy restaurant.

He tried to look into her eyes. "I'm sorry. You're right. Maybe I should go date wild women until I learn how to treat a lady. Or, lock myself in after dark." He couldn't look at her. He started moving away from the only woman he'd ever been crazy about. He had a feeling he'd be addicted to her the rest of his life.

Without a word she relaxed in his arms as he said gently, "We need to sleep now. From this moment I will not feel alive unless you are near."

Cora whispered against his ear, "Why don't we begin running toward what we both want? I'm afraid, but if I step away, I will not be able to breathe."

He held her for a long while as they watched the sunrise. They both knew the world had already changed.

She rested her head on his shoulder. "You are my Noah. You always will be. How could I not love a man who plays Harry Pratt's detective game of reporting every petty crime and lets the old ladies use your counter as a locker? You let half the town steal coffee. The mailman even brings his own mug so he can steal more."

He kissed her nose. "My Cora, I'll stop all that if it bothers you."

"No, I love you for it. Don't change a thing."

He lay back with his eyes closed.

"Are you all right, Noah?" she said.

"Better than all right. You said you loved me. Did you mean it?"

"Yes. Why would I come to listen to my sister so much? I like seeing you and talking to you. I love it when we move to the stacks and talk about the new books."

"Stop!" he almost shouted. "I love you too. I just can't believe it. I want us to have a forever kind of love. I'll never leave you. If you can put up with a sister who complains, and Bear, who wanders off all the time, maybe you can put up with me."

"Should we tell anyone?"

He shook his head. "I want you all to myself for a while. But I want you to know I won't change my mind."

"Me either. I'd like to learn to make love. I'd like eating dinners together and kissing in the stacks when no one is looking. I'd like to sleep with you."

"You are off to a great start. How about we shower together and start this secret life?"

"I can't do that. I've never . . ."

He laughed. "Me either."

They grinned at each other. "What an adventure we'll have," she said.

"Are you sure?"

"I'm sure."

He felt like he smiled all the way to his toes. "Me too," he said.

Chapter 19

Reality Awakes

Monday

Dan silently climbed the steps to the loft. After showing Andi his someday home, his barn somehow seemed shallow. When they'd returned last night, he'd stepped back into his role as her bodyguard. There'd be no more kissing today. He'd shower and be gone before Andi woke. No use going back to the house and waking the whole family. He didn't think of the barn as his home. It was simply a place to sleep and store his stuff until his own house was settled.

Old books he'd read a dozen times and a hundred others that didn't hold his interest. Boxes full of clothes that he'd never put on again and hats he'd worn while searching for a place to fit in. Workout gear hung on hooks in one corner by a huge bathroom, and in another corner was a three-sided box he called his open-air closet.

The racks were lined with uniforms and a few wool coats and flannel shirts and work jeans, well-worn. That's all he needed. The Western shirts and jeans on a shelf still looked new and folded. Clothes to go out to bars or dancing. He did neither.

None of it mattered. If the barn burned, they'd just rebuild and buy the rest.

Nothing he owned was important to him.

Another hour and the sun would peek over the east horizon. Ever since he was a baby, his mom said he woke before the dawn every morning. He'd never used an alarm or a watch. He just knew the time.

He moved across the shadows in the loft and saw Andi curled in the center of his bed. He grinned. In his bed, just where he'd dreamed she might be one day. Not likely. The woman probably had *good-bye* tattooed on her shoulder.

He moved silently. She'd likely wake up if she heard a pin drop. He was surprised she hadn't come down in the night and shot him for snoring on the stairs.

She did look beautiful sleeping though. Perfect for him. Tall but powerful. Smart. The kind of woman who'd love full-out, he bet. Unfortunately, she probably hated hard too.

As he watched her sleep now, he saw the beauty of her. Long golden hair she usually kept in a bun covered his pillow. Tan legs and arms he could see without her jeans and sweater. The gown his mother had given her was draped over a chair and she'd chosen one of his T-shirts from his top drawer. It was too big, but it molded against her body.

How could he want a woman who spent half her day hating him? He must be a masochist.

Most of the time she thought he was dumb, clumsy, and lazy. She'd asked him once why he didn't have any goals in life. No one at the age of thirty just wanted to be a deputy in a town with one stoplight. After sharing his someday house with her, she'd seen both sides of him. She probably wondered which was the dream and which was the real Danny Davis.

He couldn't tell her he'd hung all his dreams on one life, one woman. Even eight years passing didn't dull the pain sometimes. It was the memory that hung around like a shadow darkening his world.

But lately something had changed. Since Andi appeared, Danny woke up smiling.

The nights spent watching over her were interesting, but the excitement of last night left him drained. He felt the load of always being on guard. He just wanted to rest for a while.

Dan opened the window wider and lay down beside her wearing only his jeans. He thought he might rest a few minutes. If she wiggled, he'd move to the chair. One hour more of sleep would be enough. Just one hour. She'd never know he was so nearby.

As his eyes closed his hand brushed her hair and he smiled thinking that Andi's hair was the only part of the woman he dared touch again.

Far away, thunder rumbled and the low clouds kept any sign of daybreak at bay for a few more minutes. As he slipped back to sleep, he thought he felt her press against him. In more instinct than thought, he curled his arm around her and pulled her closer.

She was safe in his arms. He could rest.

Half into a dream he heard her make a little sound almost like a contented cat.

The sun would rise and warm them soon, but for now they slept. His last thought was, *She fits perfectly against me.*

A northern wind blew in beneath the clouds, promising rain. The open shutters rattled, waking them.

Dan braced for the firestorm that would come when she noticed him in the bed.

"What time is it?" she said as she raised her head an inch off the pillow.

Dan brushed the strands of her hair away from her face. "A little after seven. Breakfast isn't until eight at the house."

She dropped her head back on his arm. "Don't say a word. Don't move. I'm not ready to wake up."

He pulled the blanket over them. "Sleep, Andi. I'll watch over you."

Without opening her eyes, she moved her hand atop his heart and without a word the sorrow that had lived in him for years drained out.

When someone opened the barn door below the loft, Dan slipped from his warm bed. He moved to the closet and put on his uniform. When Karly's tiny picture came into his view, he ripped it off without hesitation. He stared at the stain where the tape had been. It would probably always be there, just like the memory of her. He glanced at Andi's sleeping form, and realized the pain was no longer there.

"I wish you a wonderful life, Karly. I know you're no longer in my future," he whispered.

As he dropped the picture and watched the past float down to the bottom of his closet, he felt like an anvil had been lifted from his heart. Danny stared at Andi and smiled. He finally had the possibility of a new path for the future.

He was putting on his boots when Digger's head appeared from the opening to the steps.

Dan decided he should put a door on the loft. Then, everyone might stop coming into his almost bedroom. And he and Andi could sleep in peace.

Of course, the chances that she'd stay for another sleep-over were zero.

Digger spider-crawled into the loft using both his hands and legs.

"Morning, Danny, my boy. I figured you'd be up here watching over our lady. It's about time for breakfast at the big house. The bunkhouse food wasn't great. I only went back for seconds twice. I was saving room for your mother's cooking."

Andi stepped out of the bedroom area wearing jeans, his

T-shirt, and a ponytail. She stared at them and frowned. "What are you two doing here?"

Digger stood at attention. "We are on guard. No one is going to kidnap you while we're your bodyguards."

Dan closed his eyes, expecting Andi to say something like *One of you is getting a little too close.* But she didn't.

He opened one eye. She wasn't even looking at him. Maybe he just dreamed that she was cuddling. No way, his dreams had never been that good.

Reaching into his closet, he grabbed one of his Western shirts, long sleeved. Flannel. "This will be warm until we go back for your clothes."

"This looks new. I can't . . ."

"You can. My mother and every one of my sisters give me Western clothes for Christmas. They seem to think if I dress like a cowboy, I'll find a girl."

"How is it working?" Digger asked. "I may never have married, but I've gone out with my share of women in my time. I could give you some pointers, son. For one, start winking. Girls may giggle at it but they take a good look at you. Next when you dance with them, move your hand a little, you know low on the waist, almost to a hip. And then there is a lot to learn about the lighting—"

Dan raised his hand like a stop cop. "Don't give me pointers until I get a pen and paper so I can write them down."

Digger nodded as Dan fought down a laugh.

When Andi showed up wearing his shirt, she walked past them without a word.

As Digger followed, he told Dan, "You should have paid her a compliment. Women love that."

As they walked to the house Digger kept doling out advice, Andi didn't say a word for once, and Dan wondered if she was the same woman who'd patted his heart this morning and kissed him as if she'd been as starved as he was.

The sky was cloudy, and for a change he didn't care. It

would be a long day with Digger talking to mostly himself and Andi not talking at all.

He leaned close to her and whispered, "You look great in my shirt."

She stayed close and whispered back, "Your snore sounds just like the AC in my apartment."

Dan decided he didn't need that pen and paper after all. But his body remembered the feel of her beside him and he figured it would be a long while before he forgot her, even if she wasn't his kind of woman. He was sunshine and laughter; Andi was storm and thunder.

Well, he guessed if sunshine and laughter didn't work out, maybe he should stand in the rain for a while.

When he held the kitchen door for her, she frowned.

He just shrugged. Good manners were good manners, even if they annoyed her.

Inside he nodded at his mother and sat down next to Andi. His knee bumped hers and she bumped him back. Then both smiled.

"Aren't you a little old for the coyote game?" she asked.

He bumped her knee again. "Aren't you?"

Dan got two bites of breakfast before the sheriff called.

He stepped out in the hall and said, "What's going on?"

The sheriff started talking double time. "It's going nuts around here. I got two waterlogged outlaws in jail. One claims he was taking a walk and got caught up in trouble. The other two we found said they were hunting for deer. Apparently, no one ever told them that no one hunts deer with a handgun.

"Two of the gang are in the hospital. One of them panicked and shot himself in the leg. The other almost drowned. It seems he'd never learned to swim."

Dan broke into Pecos's rant. "That leaves two or three, if one stayed with their cars."

"Yeah, the smart ones. My guess is they are calling in back-up. They're hiding somewhere in the county and they're planning to come after Andi. If they found her at Digger's place yesterday, they'll keep looking. I'm guessing we've got five hours to make her disappear before reinforcements. They know what she looks like and she has a bounty on her head, so we need to keep her out of sight. They've probably seen you hanging around her. But they shouldn't know she's Jamie Morrell's daughter or has two brothers. I might have told Noah at the bookshop, but he's a listener, not a talker."

Dan was making plans as he walked the hallway. "I could drive over three hundred miles in five hours," he offered. "Or I could talk to my farmhands. We have a dozen men who could stand cover at every gate. She'll be safe at my place."

Dan guessed Pecos was shaking his head. "That would put your whole family in danger."

Neither argued.

The sheriff's voice came low. "Bring her in."

"We're on our way to the office, Sheriff. I'll be there in twenty." He placed his hand on her back to hurry Andi on and one second later he was running to keep up.

Digger followed with a breakfast burrito in each hand. "Don't forget me!" he yelled.

Andi opened the passenger door of the pickup and slid across the seat until her leg hit Dan's.

"Sorry," he said low, but neither moved apart.

Digger ate as Dan drove as fast as his old pickup could go. Once, he rested his hand on Andi's leg. She didn't move away.

"You all right?" he asked while Digger kept talking between bites.

"Yes," she responded.

Dan grinned. The woman who resisted or questioned everything he did or said didn't move when he touched her. He figured that could only mean one thing. *The world was about to fall off its axis.*

He might as well live a bit during the last minutes before

bullets started zinging again. He slid his hand down almost to her knee and then moved halfway back up.

"You sure you're all right heading to town?"

She didn't look at him. "Your family doesn't need my kind of trouble."

Dan patted her jeans-covered leg and waited for the world to end.

Pecos was waiting when Dan and Andi stepped into the sheriff's office.

The sheriff swore, something he never did. "This week is starting off bad. The way it's going I'll age ten years by Friday."

They all marched toward the back. "There are only three roads out of the valley and I guess the shooters have all of them covered. Or they've already got your pickup bugged, along with all four of our county cruisers." The sheriff didn't offer anyone a chair.

Digger hurried in behind Dan and Andi. As soon as all four were in the back, Digger was busy eating as many donuts as he could while the others planned.

Finally, the old man said between mumbling bites, "The Jeep you rented seems permanently parked at my office. I could fill it and load up Andi's things left back at the cabin, and she'd be ready to go. They'll think I'm taking her stuff to her. Then, I'll vanish down those dirt roads around Someday Valley. It will be hours for them to find their way out. That will be one less bad guy you'll have to worry about. Then I'll double back and take up being Andi's bodyguard again."

"Good idea." Pecos looked surprised at Digger's plan.

Digger's temper flared. "Listen, boy, I didn't waste my time going to college. I went to war. I learned a few things. Pick them off one by one. Right now is a great time. They are scattered."

"I think we should get Andi away somewhere safe, first," Dan said.

THE WILD LAVENDER BOOKSHOP / 159

No one added anything, so Digger took over.

"And another thing, I've got listening ears. I heard Bear tell me once years ago that there was a secret way out of the valley somewhere along the rim. Apaches used it to run to safety during the Indian Wars. Most folks think it's just a legend, but it might be true. The lady who lives on Holly Rim Farm keeps a shotgun ready just in case anyone steps on her place. I think if there is a secret passage, my guess is it's on her land."

Pecos began walking down the hall between his office and the back door. "If the gunmen who shot at Andi last night stayed in town, I'd bet they've got at least one man watching Main, and he saw you come in here. They'll think Andi is in my office for safety. That's the obvious assumption. If she left town, she'd be a sitting duck."

The sheriff continued pacing and for no reason Digger followed.

Pecos issued his orders to Andi in a low voice. "In a few minutes you slip out the back and break into the back door of the bookshop if you have to. I'll find Bear and meet you there. Third floor. It's a big junk room but we can see the whole town from there. If they come for us, we'll be ready."

As Andi moved toward the back, Pecos said to the deputy, "If they can't get to her, Dan, they'll go after her family. I've heard cartels will kill a whole generation as a warning to others."

"Lucky her family is in Europe." Danny relaxed a little. "She told me her father was on his last deployment before he retires to a desk job in Washington."

The sheriff was silent for one long minute. He looked at Andi.

Pecos said, "Her brothers are back in Honey Creek. They know little about her, but they want to meet her. And this may be the only chance they ever get. If I heard they returned, the drug gang could find them too."

Andi pushed between the two men. "I'm standing right here, guys, and I don't need either of you to help me disappear.

The only reason I'll play along with your plan is I want to meet my brothers and make sure they are safe. Then, I'll vanish and never come back."

"No," Dan said.

Playfully, she pretended to punch the deputy in the stomach as a silent hint to stop ordering her around.

She tried to glare him into silence.

The sheriff ignored their exchange and continued. "Dan, meet us at the bookshop as soon as you know she's not being followed. I'll make sure the bookshop is safe. We can plan from there."

Pecos started to say something, but stopped. She wasn't under his command.

She added, "If you are late with the guy named Bear, I'm vanishing and I'm taking this deputy with me." She straightened. "Have someone like that dispatcher drive off in Danny's old pickup in a few minutes. Tell her to park it over at the Exxon with the other rusted trucks where no one will notice." She turned to Digger. "And you, soldier, ride with the dispatcher as a guard."

"Will do." Digger saluted Andi and then turned to the dispatcher and yelled across the office. "I'll get you somewhere safe, Doris. You're too valuable to leave here."

The woman wiggled out of her chair and put her headset on the desk. "I got the calls that might come in here routed to my cell. Wherever I am, I'm still on the clock," she said as she shoved snacks and a Diet Coke in a huge purse. "I'm ready. A mobile 911."

Andi didn't bother to look at Danny when she told the sheriff, "I'll meet you at the bookstore but I go separately. We will be safer if we each go alone, both to the bookshop and to wherever my brothers live."

Both the sheriff and the deputy said no at the same time.

"Yes! It is better for all of us. But first, I want my brothers safe, then when the time comes I'll vanish." She turned to

Danny, but her words were for the sheriff. "Danny will watch after them until this danger is over. I can take care of myself. If I leave, the men looking for me will leave."

The sheriff said no again, but he and Dan both saw she was making sense. The echo of her words "I can take care of myself" seemed to bounce off the walls. She was trained, she was an expert, she was right.

Danny followed her to the back door. He grabbed a raincoat with a hood off a hook by the back door and handed it to Andi. "Pecos says you might need this. Don't know why; it looks like it's slowing to a sprinkle."

Dan moved close. "Straight to the bookstore. I'll call to tell Noah to unlock the back door. Be careful."

"I will. I always am. I'll be no more than a shadow passing over the land."

He brushed the back of one finger against her cheek. "I'll be fifteen minutes behind."

Then before he let reason take over, he kissed her. Not a peck. Not a goodbye kiss. A *later, babe* kiss.

He straightened and didn't say a word. Probably, for the first time in her life, Andi seemed unable to say a thing. Like a soldier, she turned and vanished.

The sheriff was on the phone.

Danny didn't move as he listened for a shot. No sound. He counted slowly, one . . . two . . . three . . . four . . . five . . . six . . . seven . . . eight . . . nine . . . ten. He let out the breath he'd been holding. She was in the bookstore by now and he'd be with her in fifteen minutes. All he had to do was to find Bear.

He heard the rattle of his old pickup. Doris and Digger had left out the front. The plan was in motion.

Danny left in the sheriff's car while Pecos called in backup.

Chapter 20

Separated

Andi strolled slowly behind the big building toward the bookshop's back door. Three steps away from the door she heard the lock click open. She knew Danny had called Noah.

She watched the river for a minute while reviewing the plan.

Digger was with the chubby dispatcher, driving toward the four-store shopping mall. Andi guessed the sheriff wanted the seniors away from danger. They were in Danny's pickup. If Digger detected anyone following them, or rather following Danny's old pickup, he'd let the dispatcher off near the food court and head toward Someday Valley thirty miles away. Then he'd drive the rough roads until he lost his tail. Next, he'd head back to the cabin Andi had been staying in. In ten minutes, there would not be a sign that Andi was ever there.

If Digger was lucky, he would keep one outlaw busy for a while. Before the gang could call in backup, Andi would probably be a hundred miles away.

The way Andi saw it, there was one hole in the plan. Digger and the dispatcher looked nothing like Andi and Dan, but in raincoats with umbrellas no one could clearly see them. Everyone hoped the outsiders that tailed the pickup stayed busy for a while.

Her deputy said he would make sure the sheriff was sitting outside in front of the bookshop before he climbed into Pecos's car to pick up Bear. If the man wasn't in his repair shop or the café on the square, no one had any knowledge where he'd be. Everyone knew he never answered his phone except during business hours and sometimes not even then.

Andi had heard Danny tell Pecos, "I've got a hint of exactly where Bear Buchanan is. I'll be back in fifteen. Make sure no one goes in that bookshop except Noah until I get back. I told him to text both of us if anyone even tries to look in the window." Danny lowered his tone, "With Noah inside and you on the bench outside, Andi will be safe while I go get Bear."

The sheriff had nodded. "I'll have a deputy parked behind the building and one parked out front of the station until all the others are there."

When the sheriff's phone rang, Dan vanished without answering any questions. Andi didn't understand why Pecos picked the bookshop to meet, but she knew Dan needed to find Bear.

Another question bothered Andi: How could she disappear from Honey Creek and find a secret way out of the valley without anyone noticing anything or getting hurt?

As she slipped into the back of the bookshop, shadows seemed to huddle around her. The rainy day turned a calm space into something like the opening of a horror film.

Silently she watched Noah almost dancing as he hurried up a few stairs and offered his hand to someone coming down. The woman behind him was laughing as she appeared from above. Just as they stepped into the foggy light, each turned, one left to the street and the other to the door to the right, the bookstore.

The couple stopped, kissed, then went their separate ways. Both were smiling.

Andi stood in the stacks as she watched the bookshop owner make coffee, then dust. Finally, he checked the lock on the front door.

Noah showed no surprise when he turned and saw Andi near the back of the store.

"Morning," he said. "Want a cup of coffee? It's fresh."

Andi studied him. "Who are you?" The quiet owner of a little bookstore who dances down his stairs and kisses a lover goodbye. He hadn't hesitated to open the back door so he could shelter trouble. He handled love and danger like a young James Bond.

Noah grinned. "I'm a friend, if you need one."

For the first time in her life, it occurred to her that she might need help. There was no airport to fly out of, no car that worked for a fast getaway, no Pop she could talk to, fewer cops than bad guys, and two brothers she didn't know, who were in danger.

Andi laughed out loud as she thought, *And a huge deputy who is sweet on me.*

She should have stayed in Dallas. There are places to hide out in a big city. She should have waited until she testified, then come to meet her half-brothers.

She looked into Noah's intelligent eyes. "You mean that? It could turn dangerous. I can't tell you any facts."

"I'll do all I can. Danny told me that you are his girl and you are in trouble. That is all I have to know. He told me to hide you." He made sure the doors were locked, flipped a sign that said BE BACK IN 5 and held out his hand to her.

Andi took it like a lifeline. In less than twenty-four hours she'd been shot at, run for her life, hidden in a barn with animals, and been kissed by a deputy.

Why not let a bookstore owner tell her where to hide?

Chapter 21

Secrets

Danny hesitated at the back door of the sheriff's station. Every cell in his body wanted to run to Andi. He could tell himself it was to watch over her, but it was more than that. He wanted to be with her, in trouble or at peace. But he realized if there was a back way out of the valley, Bear might be the only one who knew where it was. It was Danny's duty to get her away from danger. His feelings or his fears didn't matter. She had to be safe first and this secret path on Holly Rim might be her only way.

Maybe they'd have another time when they'd be just a man and a woman who were attracted to each other. He'd promised he would hold her in a smoky bar and sway to country music. He almost laughed. It would probably be at her goodbye party. He'd hold her close and think of what could have been. They might be fighting trouble now but, in the back of his mind, he was already holding her and dreaming of making love with a woman with fire in her eyes.

Danny headed for the sheriff's car. Not his cruiser, but Pecos's own. Kid seats, candy stuck to the window and toys everywhere.

He planned to circle and head out east, not west. Then he'd take a dirt road behind the high school. Pass the abandoned train station and circle west. He'd end up on 45, which led to three farms.

County Road 45, the shortest road in the county. Six miles past the town square was the first farm, or you could call it a tiny ranch. Eliza Dosela's place was called Holly Rim. She lived alone and was seldom seen. Half a mile from the road, surrounded by trees, were a few barns and one cabin. She raised horses, sold holly at Christmas to florists for a hundred miles around. Folks said her grandfather built a sturdy fence, not to keep the horses in but to keep people out.

Bear's family settled within sight of Holly Rim but on the other side of the road where the land was pasture, perfect for farming. Bear's place reminded Dan of a children's story about a happy farm. If Eliza's land was like a book too, it would be dark and scary.

Miles further down the county road was Danny's family's place. Acres of land his two older brothers farmed and twice the grazing land for the cattle. Bear's and Eliza's places seemed small compared to the Davis operation.

Because Eliza Dosela hid away on her land and Bear never visited Dan's family farm, Danny barely knew the neighbors he passed every day. The farmers waved and knew they'd be there if the others ever needed help.

Dan's brother said once that Eliza Dosela would be ten years dead before anyone noticed.

Maybe Digger was right. There might be a safe way out of the valley on her land, and if anyone might know about it, it would be her neighbor across the road, Bear Buchanan.

All Dan had to do was find Bear and ask him. After all, he'd seen Bear driving off her land years ago.

If a passage led out of the valley and Andi could follow it without anyone seeing her, it might keep her safe. Anyone hunting her would watch the three main roads.

Dan smiled. Bear wasn't the only one who could keep secrets. Hell, he kept a little secret by accident.

Back in high school all he knew was a strange woman lived there alone. They said she had Apache blood and it was her grandfather who wrote legends of his people.

He'd heard rumors. Some said she was a witch; others said she was a writer like her grandfather only she kept her pen name secret.

When the grandfather's books were burned years ago, the family stopped coming to town. They drove fifty miles to buy supplies. They only sold their horses in Fort Worth. Now and then, someone would see the Holly Rim one-ton truck heading through town. She rarely stopped.

After Eliza was born to a mother in her forties, the family became hermits.

No one ever saw them except near Christmas when the family delivered holly to the town square. Eliza continued the tradition even after her parents died. Only the holly was delivered at midnight. Some say she was crazy, but Dan figured she just liked to be alone.

The secret Dan kept was what he'd seen on his way to school. It was a foggy dawn years ago. Danny saw Bear turning out of her gate.

He slowed and watched Bear pass the gate then stop to lock it. Bear, who usually just nodded a greeting, had visited her. And, Dan guessed, he must visit her often if he had a key to get in.

He meant to ask his father about it, but there were a hundred more important things to wonder about when you're sixteen.

Danny had forgotten about that day he'd seen Bear leaving Holly Rim. He told himself Bear might have been helping out. But, if he had a key to her gate, he might be her friend. As Danny grew, another idea drifted through his mind. She lived alone. He lived alone. Maybe they were lovers.

He never asked anyone. He might like to listen to gossip but he never said anything about others. As a kid in high school, Danny didn't think about it, but a man in his twenties considered it. They might be morning coffee-drinking friends or longtime lovers.

As he drove down the county road toward the three farms, he tried to think of what to say to Bear. The morning was foggy as it had been ten years ago. He wouldn't mention the memory. He might never know if Eliza and Bear were lovers, but he'd sensed they were friends.

And neighbors help their neighbors.

He turned in at Bear's place and circled the front and back of the house. His truck with two-feet-tall letters printed on the sides—I CAN FIX IT—wasn't parked on the farm. Bear had owned the same truck for over twenty years. It hadn't been parked at the café or sitting in front of his shop. He wasn't on his farm. Dan decided he'd look one other place before he went back to town.

Bear had to be at Holly Rim.

Danny wasn't surprised to find the gate locked.

He could wait, but that meant Andi was in danger longer. He could go back to Bear's shop and leave a note on the door, but if he wasn't answering his cell, he wouldn't find it.

Bear usually was at his shop around nine. But this morning he was late. If Bear was on his way to work, Dan would have passed him going to town.

As Danny waited at the gate at Holly Rim, he looked up near the trees and saw two people on horses racing toward the cabin. The man was big and the lady small with her long hair flying.

Their laughter floated on the wind.

The deputy knew the moment they saw him. The woman turned to the barn and the big man headed straight toward the gate and Dan.

Bear was five feet away when he slowed and said, not too friendly, "What do you want, Dan? This better be important!"

"Yes, sir." Dan suddenly turned into a kid. Bear had never said a mean word to him, but he'd never been friendly either. "We've got trouble and we need your help."

Bear stepped down off his horse. He slowly looped the reins over the gate as he seemed to be making up his mind to go or stay. One glance at the cabin, then he nodded, but he didn't look happy.

The deputy smiled. Come to think of it, Bear never looked happy.

In three steps Bear climbed the fence with the ease of a twenty-year-old.

"You on sheriff business, Deputy?"

"Private business. What I need to say is between me and you and a woman I care for. She's law enforcement, hiding here until she has to testify. She's in real danger. We were shot at last night over at Digger's lodge."

"Why did you come looking for me here, boy?"

"I saw you at this gate once, years ago." Dan almost added that he wasn't a boy, but Bear would probably slug him.

"You tell anyone?"

"No, sir. Not my business."

The two men stared at each other. Both were strong but Bear was almost thirty years older. Standing two feet apart Dan noticed he was taller than Bear. The man Dan had always thought was a giant was shorter than he was. In that moment the two men understood one another. Dan nodded once in respect and Bear did the same.

Bear headed toward the car. "If you need me, I'm in. A man who doesn't ask but one favor in twenty years need not to ask but once. Fill me in on the way to town. When it's over I'm guessing I'm to never mention what's about to happen to anyone."

"Yes. Tell no one. My lady's life may depend on it." Dan followed Bear and climbed in the sheriff's car. "Are you going to tell Miss Eliza you're leaving?"

"She'll know when she sees the horse tied here. She'll take

care of the pinto. I'll help all I can, but you'll bring me back when we're finished."

"Yes, sir."

As Danny turned toward town, he filled Bear in on the problem. He even told Bear that using a secret passage might be the only way out of the valley without someone getting killed.

Bear barked out a laugh. "You mean your girl."

"Yes. She's my girl but she doesn't know it yet."

Chapter 22

The Reunion

Andi paced the third floor of the bookshop. There was so much dust on everything she could grow tomatoes. It had been sixteen minutes and Dan wasn't with her. Neither was the sheriff. Both promised they'd follow her to the bookshop.

If the station was hit by the men who wanted her dead, she should have been there.

"No. Didn't happen," she said to the silence. She would have heard shots from next door.

Maybe they were called out on a wreck. Another *no* echoed off the silent walls. Either the sheriff or Dan, or even Digger, would stay behind to guard her. These men, grown in the heart of Texas, were brave and determined and dumb to think she couldn't take care of herself.

Andi thought of one other thing the deputy was. He was lovable.

She decided to give them a few more minutes as she sat down on a huge old desk. She began to think. Somehow, she'd lost control of her life. If she'd not come to this town, if she hadn't let Dan take her to his place last night, she wouldn't have kissed him or cuddled with him. She should have stayed in Dallas. She should have fought her own fight on turf she knew, and come to meet her brothers later when all was calm.

Snuggling with the deputy meant nothing, she told herself. She'd just been cold. But, for a blink, she remembered how good it felt. He cared about her but she couldn't get involved. She knew when she started this dangerous career, she'd always be alone.

She needed to make her own plan. Too many people were involved. Someone might get hurt. She was in hiding in the middle of town with only a bony bookstore owner to bar the door. Surely, she could come up with a better strategy. The more people involved in her problem, the more people who might get hurt.

Andi reached for her weapon strapped to her ankle. She checked to make sure it was loaded. Two bullets left. She felt she was about to go into a sword fight with a pocketknife.

She liked Noah and he made good coffee but the man was a thinker, not a fighter. She'd bet he didn't even own a gun.

Andi hated this. She was a runner, a fighter, a risk-taker, not someone who hid away like a rat.

Suddenly footsteps seemed to thunder outside the door. Three people were climbing the stairs fast. Her only choice was to hide.

She slipped under the desk and waited. From the noise she guessed that men were coming as fast as they could. Coming to kill her or to tell her she was safe. She wouldn't know until the door was opened.

Only two bullets. She needed another weapon.

She felt around under the huge office desk with every other drawer missing. Dust everywhere. Old yellow newspapers. A few thin books taped to the underside of the desk so long ago they threatened to fall. Three *Playboys* open with pages missing. An empty beer bottle and several candy wrappers. Two

Coke cans with candles pushed into the opening. It occurred to her this might be the R-rated section of the bookshop.

The invaders stomped and slowed. They were on the third floor. The doorknob slowly turned.

Andi stood, feet wide apart. Arms straight out. Elbows locked. Finger on the trigger. She took a breath and slowly advanced. She'd die, but the first two men who entered wouldn't be around to spend the money for her killing.

The door rattled open and a kid of about fifteen jumped in. Dark hair. He was breathing fast and hard. When he saw her, he froze, then slowly raised his hands as if he'd seen a hundred gangster movies. His wide gray eyes looked like they were in danger of falling out.

"Don't move," she said as she lowered the weapon. The kid's gaze followed the gun.

"Breathe, kid." She holstered her firearm as she heard the sheriff yelling her name.

Suddenly it sounded to Andi like another stampede rushing up the stairs, but she had to deal with these three first.

"Who are you?" she shouted at the boy.

He couldn't get a word out. Hands up, not breathing, and staring at Andi like she was an alien.

Keeping her eyes on the teenager, she saw a man in a suit out of the corner of her eye. He stepped inside the room holding a suitcase over his heart as he moved wide to the left. His voice was familiar. The lawyer. "He's your little brother, Andi. I found him just like I said I would."

She turned to the lawyer she'd spoken with weeks ago on the phone. "Jackson, right. You're sure he is my brother?"

"He is," a stranger said as he moved between her and the kid. "He's my brother, too."

Andi felt like everyone in the room was speaking a foreign language. She couldn't even get a word in as the kid and his bigger brother introduced themselves at lightning speed.

The room suddenly fell silent. The offspring of Jamie Morrell just stared at one another.

The sheriff slowly opened the storage room door and frowned liked he missed the start of a show.

The only one who seemed willing to talk was the lawyer. He explained that Andi was in danger and it would be good if all of them vanished for a few days while the sheriff could make sure the men who shot at her last night were gone.

Suddenly Rusty, her newfound older brother, started asking questions.

"Where'd you come from?"

"Why are men chasing you?"

"How come you didn't come see us before?"

The kid said to his brother, "She doesn't have gray eyes."

Rusty glanced at the lawyer and added, "Didn't you tell us she was a guy?"

The kid broke into the questions to explain a fact to this big brother. "Maybe she was a man, Rusty. I heard some guys just cut . . ."

"Shut up," everyone in the room shouted. Rusty looked embarrassed. The sheriff frowned as if trying to figure out who to shoot, and Andi decided she loved this kid.

Both new brothers moved close to her as if they were her bodyguards.

Andi opened her mouth to tell Rusty a "one-minute brother" can't boss her around, but she looked at the kid. He was in need of a haircut and had two dirty Band-Aids on his right hand and both her new brothers' clothes were worn and in need of care.

Andi logged the facts. No woman in their lives. They were tall but bone thin, and the younger one didn't look like he could talk to the opposite sex. Like they were stray cats, and Andi wanted to adopt them.

The kid just stared at her.

Andi winked at him and he smiled. Then one tear rolled

down his sunburned cheek. "You could have died before I ever met you," he said in a shaky voice. "In the will, we thought you were a brother. Last year, when I came to town, I didn't have any kin. Then I found Rusty, and now you showed up and I've got two. Maybe even three, if the last one comes along."

The "almost a man" wrapped his arms around her and forced himself not to cry as he kept saying, "I got a sister."

Andi patted Zach's back as she looked around. Rusty and the sheriff were talking while the lawyer seemed to be patting himself on the back. Random questions bounced off the walls but no one was answering.

She was in real trouble. She had a little brother worried about her and a big brother who seemed to think he was in charge of her. The sheriff was threatening to lock them all up for their safety.

Andi closed her eyes. Questions circled the room but for once in her life Andi felt she was a part of a family.

The second wave of visitors stormed up the two flights of stairs. It sounded like troopers. There was no question one was Danny. He was calling her name as if she might not hear him coming. "Andi! Andi."

She was boiling over with emotions. When he rushed the door, she jumped into his arms. Everyone in the room laughed as books and chairs flew out of the couple's way.

The kid leaned toward his big brother and said, "Our sister must like deputies."

Rusty looked worried. "I hope she just likes one. Two deputies won't fit in our house."

Chapter 23

The Plan

Bear Buchanan slowed as the big deputy took the lead into the third-floor storage room above the bookstore.

He wasn't surprised that no one in the room noticed him slide into the shadows with the deputy storming in. Bear had no idea what was happening in the building he owned, but everyone in the room seemed to be in shock.

Bear moved around them as if all were mannequins.

Danny had pushed past two brothers and lifted a woman who was beautiful, tall, and mad. The deputy hugged her while she kicked him.

Bear almost laughed. The young deputy had told Bear he was guarding a witness. The lady left him at the sheriff's back door heading for a hideout. She had a gang of bad guys hunting her. Dan admitted he feared she'd be shot before he could get back to her. Or, she'd disappear and he'd never see her again.

From the looks of it the woman was very much alive but Bear couldn't figure out why his third-story storage room was her hiding place. Couldn't someone in the sheriff's office think of another hideout?

When Dan let her down, she smacked him a playful blow with her fist in his middle. He folded over and let out fake suffering.

Rusty, the town's best carpenter if anyone asked Bear, stepped up and faced Deputy Davis. "You may be a member of law enforcement, Dan, but don't you touch my sister unless she smiles, 'cause if you do I'll see you lose a few teeth." He lifted his fist an inch from Dan.

Bear started laughing again. Danny might be bigger, but Bear figured his money would be on Rusty in a fight. Danny was mostly writing tickets and Rusty was building houses. Fact was Bear liked both men. He might be thirty years older, but if the two men started a fight, Bear would stop it.

Before anyone moved, Andi acted. She turned to her newly found brother and yelled, "Don't you dare hurt my deputy."

Everyone froze but Bear. For the first time in years, he laughed so hard his stomach hurt. Neither man would know why they were fighting, but Bear knew why he was laughing. She might be hitting the deputy but the lady was making a claim on Danny. And from all appearances, judging by his grin, the big guy didn't seem to mind her beating on him one bit.

Bear watched the kid circle the only woman in the room and asked Rusty, "If the deputy is hers do we have to take him home too? Just feeding the guy will bankrupt us."

Meanwhile, the lady was threatening everyone but never left Dan's side. She introduced him to her brothers. Rusty had known Dan for years. They'd worked together on community projects and Dan helped Zach when he was new in town.

But Danny shook hands with Rusty and Jackson, as friends do. Bear backstepped as he usually did in crowds.

The only ones in the room not talking now were the lady and the deputy.

Rusty, a carpenter who had done some work for Bear a few times, started arguing with the sheriff the second he came through the door. He wanted Andi to come to his house. "We're taking my sister home, Pecos."

The sheriff was trying to explain that the brothers needed to disappear with the sister for a few weeks, and Rusty was claiming his house would be the place for Andi. It was so isolated the mailman couldn't find it. Rusty said the three siblings needed time to talk.

Jackson grumbled something from over by the window.

Bear frowned at the lawyer. The hideout was getting more crowded than the town square. "What are you doing here, Jackson?"

"I'm their lawyer. I saved Rusty's life one night when he rolled his car. I got Zach out of trouble when he came to town to find his kin, and I called Andi's mother to find Andi. I've been trying to give these siblings their inheritance for a year, even though they don't even want it."

Since the lawyer was on some kind of platform speech, Bear decided to do like everyone else: ignore him.

Andi wasn't listening to the sheriff or the lawyer since she was arguing with Danny. She told him he was late and he was telling her to stop using him as a punching bag.

Bear had no idea why the two were quarrelling. His best guess was it was foreplay. She was pointing at his heart and calling him names and he kept patting her a bit low on her back. They were growing louder and closer.

Finally, all the men stopped talking and just watched the couple.

Bear heard Zach tell his brother if a girl ever yelled at him that way he'd run.

Rusty answered, "It's not as simple as you think."

The sheriff finally got a word in. "Quiet!" His command rattled the dirty windows.

Andi kept poking Dan.

The deputy caught her hand and tucked it under his arm and

announced, "Bear assures me he can get out of town without being followed. But no one goes with Bear but me and her. She'll pass through the opening in the rim. Bear will guide her. Once we get to the climb, I'll remain behind to make sure no one follows."

Everyone started talking at once. Rusty said he was here to protect his sister. Zach just said, "Me too."

The lawyer demanded he should go because he was her lawyer.

The sheriff just wanted to see this secret path that folks had talked about for generations. Everyone thought it was a myth.

Bear shook his head and joined the argument. "I go, with Danny on guard. I know I can trust him with a secret. He'll only be with us until we start to climb, not all the way. I go alone with her as we near the rim. She'll be safe. I'll show her the passage."

When no one said anything, Bear added, "Her brothers will be safe if no one knows the plan but us. They can meet up with her in Dallas. They'll be safer that way."

Everyone nodded but Danny.

"Everybody understand?"

Bear saw they understood there was no room for discussion.

The sheriff nodded. "I will be sure she'll have cover until we get on the county road." He looked around the room. "Andi, I think it's safe to go with your brothers now. You three have a great deal to talk about." The sheriff pointed to the deputy. "Dan will pick you up. I'll be on the turn into Holly Rim from County Road 45, making sure no stranger passes." He looked at Andi. "Remember you, Dan, and Bear will be at Eliza's place by dawn. As soon as it's light enough you'll all be climbing. Then . . ."

Andi took over. "Draw me a map to the passage. I can take care of myself from there. I don't want to put anyone else in sight of the men trying to kill me."

No one said anything. No one liked the idea of her going it alone after she was out of the valley either, but they also knew she'd be safer if she didn't have a tail.

Bear watched the couple. The deputy sat down on the desk so he was eye to eye with her. He gently placed his hands on her waist and pulled her between his legs.

She didn't protest. In fact, she pushed closer and rested her hand over her deputy's chest.

Everyone in the room was talking and planning but the couple. They were not fighting, or yelling. They were making peace with each other. Saying goodbye. Maybe forever.

Bear realized that it didn't matter if their secret love was out of sight or for the world to see. It existed.

His little Eliza knew nothing of the plan. Maybe she'd help because a woman was in danger, but Bear was going to ask her to allow people on her land. Even if Bear stayed on the path on the other side of the rim, people would know the legend was real.

Bear was breaking his word.

His fairy might turn her back. He'd help save a woman's life, but he'd shatter his.

Chapter 24

Rainy Day Attraction

Noah watched his surprise guests leave the bookshop one by one.

The sheriff and Bear came down first. They were not talking as they went out the back and borrowed Noah's car without asking. Noah always left the keys over the visor. Bear sometimes needed to move Noah's car when he had to park a delivery truck.

Noah heard the sheriff say he needed to set some things in motion. It was going to be a long night. Noah guessed the sheriff would be assigning his men to log every car that drove down County Road 45 and also the dirt road heading to Rusty and Zach's place.

Bear mentioned that the sheriff could drop him at Eliza's place. He said it might take him all night to talk her into letting strangers on her land.

Everyone coming down seemed to have a job to do but Noah. The deputy was staying upstairs in Bear's junk room with Andi.

Noah stared outside at the town. The morning was cloudy

and not even the Over the Hill ladies were out walking the square yet. His Cora had started her day early at the grade school and knew nothing that was going on. His kiss had been fast at the door. Too fast, he thought. He'd make up for it when she got home.

He wanted to tell her all that was going on this morning, but he'd have to wait. Strange how someone who was barely a friend could turn into a lover so fast.

Lightning flashed just outside and he realized that he wanted to talk about everything with her for the rest of his life.

Noah climbed to the third floor with a broom and a trash bag. He might as well start cleaning. If he could clear a path to the desk he'd found maybe he could get Dan, the sheriff, and Rusty to help him get the desk downstairs when all this settled. He'd fix up a corner office. It was time things changed. Noah wasn't drifting through life anymore; he was planting roots, and he was planting them right here.

The danger this morning sparked an idea for a story. He wanted to write all that had happened, or what he imagined could have happened. The story forming in his mind might go any direction.

His creativity was growing inside him. Freedom was bouncing around without boundary. He'd start with a short story of how each player slipped into the bookstore and what they had to plan, and later he'd read his story to Cora tonight.

All at once Noah's world was in color, not black and white. He didn't need to be in a big city, or travel or have adventures. He could live, really live, right here.

Two floors up Andi and Dan were looking out at the town square. All was quiet, but everyone seemed to be waiting. Each had a role in Andi's escape.

As soon as Andi's brothers called to tell her to come to their house, and Noah's car, which the sheriff had stolen to take Bear home, was back behind the building, Noah decided he'd lock the bookshop. He was going to call his parents to tell them that he was going to ask a woman to marry him.

He'd guess he wouldn't get the whole sentence out before they started yelling, demanding he come home and a hundred other things.

It didn't matter. He'd slept beside her last night and every time he'd woken up and seen her in the moonlight, she was more beautiful than the last. If they slept together for eighty years, Cora would always be beautiful.

His parents wouldn't be happy. He knew exactly what they'd say.

This isn't the right time of year to travel.

You are moving too fast.

You haven't known her long enough.

You don't have the money to afford any kids.

They'd say he had been down in Texas too long and it was time for him to come home and get a real job. He'd be a poor writer and he'd never make enough money to live.

Noah would listen, be polite, not say a word. Then he would tell them he loved them. He'd try to get home for Christmas, then for the second time in his life he would do exactly what he wanted to do.

Half an hour later Noah swept the third-floor storage room, and he made his list. Ask Cora to marry him. But don't tell Bear for a few days. The man seemed to have his hands full trying to help the deputy's girl vanish.

A thud sounded from below, on the second floor. Danny and Andi were waiting for Rusty to call and give the okay to come out.

Noah thought it was safe up there, but they shouldn't be making noise.

Another thud.

Noah smiled. Probably foreplay again.

He closed his eyes, imagining he was already sitting in the

corner desk downstairs writing. Noah could create while he watched the snow in winter and the people sitting on the benches feeding the squirrels in summer. On cold days he'd put out his store sign that said BE BACK IN 5 up and drive over to get Cora, but on nice days he'd walk over to the grade school and walk with her. They'd cook dinner after he closed up, then he'd read her what he wrote that day when the store wasn't busy, which was pretty much all the time.

Then they'd take a bottle of wine upstairs to the roof. They would watch the stars, as he held her. Of course, once his writing began to pay, they'd travel, but Honey Creek would always be home.

Reality interrupted. A third thud sounded and then laughter.

Maybe I'll add a little romance to the novel, Noah thought. After all, he was thinking of romance, and obviously the deputy and Andi were practicing it. Or fighting. With those two it could go either way.

Chapter 25

Trouble Comes to Those Who Wait

An hour later, Andi stared at the clouds outside the dirty windows of the third floor of the bookshop. It seemed more like it was lit in evening shadows than midmorning sunshine. The beautiful town of Honey Creek looked like faded photos. Andi paced across the junk piled in the storage room. Old furniture, books in no order, broken toys. In one corner, a worn-out fireman's uniform rested as if the body that once occupied it had turned to dust.

All were waiting, watching, planning. The sheriff had returned and was murmuring into his phone. The lawyer had disappeared and no one seemed to miss him, and Andi's older brother was fixing a broken chair for some reason. The temporary prisoners of the third floor were pacing, like lions in a cage.

Thirty minutes ago, they were talking, but now all seemed to move to their corners.

Andi was complaining more to herself than Danny that no one was doing anything. "I bet no one has been in this room for years except a few adolescents. Who knows where they found their reading materials?" She kicked an empty box out of her way.

Dan didn't even look like he was listening. She wasn't even sure he knew she was talking. In less than an hour her deputy had lost interest in her or anything she was saying. It seemed he was putting a puzzle together blindfolded.

It occurred to Andi that most of their conversations were arguments anyway, and she was always the one who ended up yelling. As she folded her arms and moved away from him, she had a rare glimpse into her own emotions. For a second, she felt lost and numb. She wondered when she'd hardened. She used to say she cared about people, that was why she took the tough assignments.

Once her job had been exciting. She was making the world a better place. She loved what she did, but somehow she no longer felt anything. No caring, no fear, no joy. Sometime over the years of working mostly alone she'd turned into a machine.

She saw the kid reading one of the comics that he'd found on a shelf. She wanted to feel something for him but she'd been undercover for so long, pretending to be someone else forever. She didn't know what was real anymore.

"Two brothers," she murmured. "I have two brothers."

She looked out at the park in the center of town. Logging the facts. A dozen ladies walking the square. A little girl running across the grass chasing her dog. A man with rounded shoulders and a plaid jacket apparently was acting as a crossing guard for the old ladies.

Harry Pratt.

Once she heard a name, she remembered it. The civilian cop. Maybe she'd turned into him. Running around helping people who didn't need her.

One old lady bopped Harry with her umbrella.

Not that Andi cared about the man on the street or even the deputy. She'd been trying to get rid of Dan for days, she lied to herself. She had more important things to worry about than Danny.

She had somehow let him get too close. She'd made him think she cared about him.

The moment she lied to herself she felt a pain in her chest.

A memory drifted in her mind. The deputy had curled around her and cuddled her against him.

Her skills told her that she needed to vanish, get out of danger. If she ran, the people around would be safer. The last thing she wanted to do was get involved with the locals.

But she couldn't run, not this time. This was her birthplace. These people had stayed with her, trying to help. For the first time in a long time, she was beginning to know what normal was like. A family dinner. Talking to people walking by. Teasing the deputy.

A tear rolled down her cheek. She looked at Zach, and for a moment mourned the life she could have had if she'd known she had brothers.

She walked over to the kid and put her arm around him. In another few years, he'd be a man. Until then, she'd watch over him, even if it was from a distance.

He looked up at her, confused. "Are you a person in my life that I'll only see once? Or are you gonna be around?"

She pulled him closer. "I'm going to be around. I don't know how it could happen this fast, but I love you."

Zach hugged her hard and then pulled away fast, wiping at his eyes. "Can I call you Sis?"

"I hate that name." Andi smiled. "But I guess I'm stuck with it."

From half a room away, she met Rusty's gaze and caught his wink.

"Darn, I've got two people in my life I've got to worry about now." Andi laughed.

"I already take care of myself. You don't have to watch over me. But you can bet I'm going to watch over you." Rusty crossed the room to join his kin.

Andi started to say, "I can take . . ." She stopped. No one

ever listened; she might as well give up. She turned to Zach. "There are more people you're going to want to meet. My step-father may not be my real dad, but he'd take you in and teach you all sorts of things. He's an ex-marine."

Her brothers shared a look. "Great. I guess we're going to have to build another bedroom," Rusty said.

"Can we paint it marine green?" Zach asked.

"Why not."

"He took me in. I'm sure he'll take you guys too." Andi smiled. "My mom will love you too, but I'm warning you, she can't cook."

Andi moved back to pester Danny. All these feelings were too much for her. She needed a distraction.

The deputy was the perfect target.

"I wouldn't be surprised if you hid the magazines here when you were a kid." Andi turned on Danny as she tried to push feelings away. She'd meant to tease him, but when she looked up Danny was staring at her.

She picked the nearest magazine, which happened to be *Playboy*, and hid behind it.

Andi's brothers slipped out before they accidentally got in-volved with the deputy's ribbing. Her brothers were not raised near one another but they were alike. Quiet.

Andi almost giggled. The deputy wasn't taking the bait to argue. He just stood and walked straight to her.

"I ever tell you that I love men with red hair?" She couldn't see his face. "Well, I won't."

"I figure you'll get around to it." He still didn't look at her.

She stepped closer and faced him with the *Playboy* as a bar-rier. "Think of something to do, Deputy. I never was good at stakeouts. I like the action."

"There is nothing to do, but maybe you could take your clothes off so I can compare you and this model. I'm betting you'll win," he answered as he picked another issue. "Your brothers should leave soon, so we don't have much time. It won't take them long to get ready for the plan."

He grinned. Sparks were practically flying out of her eyes.

The deputy started thumbing through another old *Playboy* magazine he'd found under the desk. When he turned the page sideways, she walked by and slapped his reading material from his hands.

He stood. She pushed him back down on the desk and a book tumbled to the floor and landed on the dirt. She picked it up. Hardback. Small, yellowed with age. She could barely read the letters. "*Legends of Our People* by Elan Dosela."

She passed it to him and sat down on the desk.

Danny turned the book over in his big hand. "Dosela is Bear's neighbor who is going to let us cross her land at dawn. I remember hearing about one of her ancestors. Folks used to claim he was a writer. Old-timers say his stories were about his people. If we get on her land maybe I'll show her this book."

He smiled and passed the treasure back to Andi. "How about reading a chapter in our story, honey?"

She lifted the cover. "Look at this," she said as she studied the text, forgetting she was still leaning against his chest. "This book must be priceless."

He settled her next to his knee and she began to read.

Andi was aware Danny was watching her as if she was the third-floor entertainment. As she read, her words began to flow faster with excitement.

"You don't wait for anything, do you, Andi? I'll bet you were born early and you're one of those readers who reads the last page first."

She looked away from the old book, thankful no one was listening. With him now sitting on the desk, they were eye to eye for once and he had just read her correctly.

"I see you, Andi. I really know you."

"You just said that so Rusty wouldn't consider beating you

up for suggesting I take off my clothes." She turned to the book again. *Big brothers protect their sisters*, she thought.

Andi smiled. She liked having a big brother. "But I can hold my own in a fight."

Dan winked. "Either you're bored or just looking for a victim. Strip and we'll fight. I'll even let you win."

She gave him that look that silently said he'd spouted something dumb, then she backed away. "We're hiding out, remember?" With her fists on her hips, she started lecturing again. Danny might be two years younger than she was, but she swore he was born yesterday.

Every time she looked at him like he was too dumb to remember to breathe, the deputy just smiled.

She moved closer. There was something touchable about a man who didn't make a pass but had "come get me" in his eyes.

Reason won out and she stepped away. "We've got to keep our heads in the game. The men looking for us won't hesitate to leave collateral damage.

"I've survived a hundred times because I can read people. I can read a man. Whether he carries a knife or a gun. Whether he'll fight or run. If he's all talk or action. And most of all, I can always tell when men lie . . ."

She moved so close her nose almost touched his. "How about I read you? You don't want to hurt anyone. You back down because you're worried about your strength. I see no fear, only worry." She studied him for a minute more.

She saw his eyes fill with sorrow. He stared deep into the corners of the room as if looking into the past.

Andi pushed. "You have hurt someone you didn't mean to. Right?"

He was silent for a moment, then said, "I did hurt someone years ago, but I'd stand in front of you and fight to keep you safe." He snorted. "Even if you are as mean as an alligator. I know it's my job, but it's more than that and we both know it is."

"For the hundredth time, I can take care of myself. But I

have to ask, Why me? Why care? I've been nothing but trouble to you, Dan."

He thought for a minute, then answered in a low voice. "Because, now and then, I see fire in your eyes. Maybe I'm waiting for one day when I'll see that fire when you look at me."

Andi wasn't used to rare honesty. "The other day you said you wouldn't start anything but you'll finish it."

He grinned. "Maybe you don't read men as well as you think you do."

The urge to slug him came to her mind, but there was another feeling. Without hesitation she leaned near and kissed him on his cheek.

Moving slow, he wrapped his arm around her shoulder, pulled her near and kissed her full-out. She was so shocked she didn't move. Danny wasn't taking; he was giving.

She'd never been kissed like this. Tender, gentle, pleasing. This was not the beginning of passion on a one-night stand. This wasn't trying to conquer or prove skill.

She wanted more, but reason won out. This game between men and women was nothing more than a tug-of-war.

When she moved away, he didn't try to stop her.

She walked across the room from him, away from allowing herself to feel. For the first time she wanted to turn around.

Danny moved to the window. His words came flat, without emotion. "The old ladies are putting on plastic rain hats about ten minutes late. They're determined to get their steps in."

Andi moved to the window. The sheriff moved into the room as a trooper pulled up by Noah's car and parked beside two other white cars. Almost a dozen women headed for more coffee.

Dan leaned forward, touching his chest against her back and wrapped his hand around hers. "I just got an idea of how we're getting you to your brothers. We split up."

"Makes sense. The gang doesn't know about them."

Dan continued, "I'll go down and look like I'm watching for you. Even ask folks outside if they've seen you."

Pecos began to listen.

The sheriff said, "I'll slip down the fire escape and come running. That should give Dan time to get you away."

"No. Andi can slip in with the walkers," Dan said.

All at once everyone was talking.

Dan held her tighter. "I'll set it up. Give everyone ten minutes to get in place. Your brothers are gone. The sheriff will make it to the station so he can run out yelling.

"While everyone is watching outside, slip downstairs and mix in with the walkers."

He moved his hands around her waist and tugged her to him one last time. "You have to disappear.

"Once you're downstairs, button up the raincoat and pull up your hood as far as you can. Go out with the ladies. One of the walkers is your height and she'll know where to take you. Tell her I said to get you out of town fast. She knows where everyone lives."

"She might not agree to this plan." Andi couldn't just go up to an old lady and ask such a favor.

"She will." Danny started downstairs. Since he had a grip on her hand, Andi came along.

"Why are you so sure, Danny?"

He grinned. "She's my granny and she's always packing. You'll be safe."

When they reached the landing, he turned. He stared at her for a minute and for once she didn't say a word.

Without a sound. Without a touch. He leaned forward and his words touched her cheek.

"I'll find you. This between us isn't finished."

She pushed the little book she'd been carrying against his heart. "Keep this for me until I see you again. I'm not finished with it, or you."

Danny pushed the book back. "No, keep it with you. You're going to Eliza's ranch. That's where it belongs."

Chapter 26

Two Hearts

Bear woke with the sun in full bloom. He growled like the wild animal he was.

He'd spent the night in the loft of the barn with his fairy. As always, he loved watching her wake. She reminded him of a swan taking flight.

Eliza would stretch as if reaching for the sky and then slowly she'd look at him like he was a surprise in her bed Christmas morning.

When he'd driven in last night, she wouldn't let him talk. She wanted her Bear.

She'd always had a hunger for him. Bear figured the heavens gave him to her because she needed a man holding a ton of love.

They always made time to mention his daughters and the town and the crops, but their meeting was a silent time alone first, a treasure between lovers.

Bear knew he had a big favor to ask of his fairy. A favor she might not give.

He'd heard her say she'd never write or even whisper the secret. It was a pledge to her people, all who'd died.

He didn't ask as he pulled her to him. Time was short. Lives were in danger, but he had to hold her as gently as he had that first day. They hadn't said a word that first night he came to her. Emotion flowed too strong. He was afraid then also. He'd just held his arms out then and waited. She'd said she'd seen all his love in his eyes.

She'd run full out to her Bear and was in flight when he caught her.

The moment her heart rested against his he'd known he'd never love another.

Andi's life was in danger, Danny's love might be shattered, the sheriff's men would fight for what was right. So would Bear, but he did not know if his fairy would be beside them.

And Bear knew he couldn't demand she break an oath.

When he'd stretched out on his blanket and she floated her mother's quilt over them, he knew something was different. She must have sensed it for Bear saw a drop of fear in her soft brown eyes.

"You know, my fairy, that you are the reason my heart beats. If you die before me, I'll dig two graves up on the rim and lie beside you."

She was still for a while with her hand holding two of his fingers, then she said, "Well, if you're going to bury your big body on my land, I might as well marry you. My ancestors will not like it but you'll grow on them in the hereafter."

He burst out laughing and hugged her. "You mean it?" He howled.

For a while they didn't think of anything but one another. She'd said yes.

Just after dawn, Bear stood at the doorway and looked up at the rim, hoping their plan would work. Only one piece was still missing, the most important one, and time was running out. No one but Eliza knew the way to the cave that passed through the rim.

He could see his fairy walking her land, thinking. She knew something was up but hadn't asked him what. She was worrying about the unknown.

The silence was broken by the rattle of a pickup over a caliche road. About fifty feet out, the truck stopped, and one woman got out.

Dan stayed in his cab and Bear stood by his corner of the house. They knew what was about to happen needed to be between the two women.

Bear could tell that his fairy was uncomfortable with a stranger on her land, but she walked forward to meet Andi and asked, "How can I help you?"

Andi answered in short sentences as if she was reading a police report. Bear heard her say, "I need your help. I need to cross your land through the secret pass I've heard of, if it really exists. My life depends on it."

Eliza shook her head. "Only Apaches know about that. Only a few told the secret and they've all died."

"There must be another way out."

"I can't. I would be betraying my parents and my people and my oath. I promised to never tell that secret."

The detective nodded and Bear watched the plan to get Andi out safely crumble. He looked to Dan, and the big man's head was resting on his steering wheel. His future with Andi was slipping away.

She straightened, offered her hand, and said, "I understand and respect your decision. I'll keep fighting. There's bound to be another way." She patted her pocket, searching for something, and slowly pulled out a small book. She handed it to Eliza. "I understand why you can't help me, but this belongs to you. I found it taped to the bottom of an old desk for safety. I don't know who hid it, but I'm guessing it'll be safe with you."

Tears began to fall down Eliza's cheeks as she realized what a gift Andi was giving her. She clutched the book to her chest and turned to the rim. "Thank you, ancestors. You've shown me the way." She looked back to Andi, pulling a ring from her finger. She handed it to the detective. "You are now my sister. I'll take you up, through the rim."

Andi said, "I have nothing to give you."

Eliza smiled. "You've already given me back my lost heritage."

Bear signaled Dan to follow him to the barn and called, "We've got to saddle the horses."

The deputy stepped out of the pickup with a rifle in his hand. "We'll stand guard. If anyone comes through the gate, they better be yelling who they are."

Neither man looked at his woman. Bear couldn't stand to see sorrow and fear in his fairy's eyes. And he knew Danny wasn't ready to say goodbye to the woman he loved.

Chapter 27

Liberation

The phone rang. Noah glanced at the clock to see that it was six in the morning, 8:00 a.m. New York time. No one would be calling that early but his parents. He picked up the cell phone and slipped from bed, trying not to wake Cora.

How he hated leaving her warmth. Three steps took him to the living room where he could see the number, and dread curled up his spine. "Morning, Mom. What's wrong?"

"You know what is wrong. I got your message. My only child has lost his mind. How could he think of marrying a woman we haven't even met?"

He moved to the window and spent a minute watching the town sleep before he spoke. "Mom, you're going to love her."

Her voice rose in panic. "How could I possibly like an old maid in her thirties who's trying to steal my son? She probably has the vocabulary of a first-grader. Texans never know how to talk."

Noah closed his eyes and said calmly, "Mom, I'm going to marry her."

A long pause hung on the line.

Then his mother's voice shook with anger. "Your father and I have talked it over. If you marry her, you are no longer our son."

"You can't mean that."

"We do mean it. We're not going to spend the rest of our lives driving back and forth across the country. And I would worry myself into an early grave."

Noah closed his eyes, no longer wanting to see the sunrise.

He realized in that moment that he was free.

He was not his parents' child. He was Cora Lee Buchanan's lover and partner for life. He opened his eyes and looked at his town. Deep inside he felt sorry for his parents. They had already missed so much of life, and now they were cutting off more joy they could've had.

He straightened and smiled and realized he was ready to step in and take all the happiness he could get. "I'm sorry you feel that way, Mom. I'll talk to you next week."

As he hung up the phone, snapshots of his childhood tumbled from his memory, giving him a different perspective.

Silently, he moved back to the bedroom and snuggled beside Cora. "I love you; I always will. I've been waiting for you all my life."

Half asleep, Cora kissed his cheek. "I love you too. I never knew there was a man like you out there for me." Yawning, she asked, "Who was that call from so early in the morning?"

"My parents. Mom talked but you can bet my dad was listening on the other line."

"What did they need?"

"Nothing important. I told them I was going to be a writer."

"What did they say?"

"Nothing." He realized, for the first time really, that this was his life, and he planned to live it on his terms with beautiful Cora by his side. He kissed her cheek like she'd done his. "What's on the calendar today?"

"I was supposed to meet Katherine for our lunch with Bear, but he's not here."

Noah sat up and rested his back against the headboard. "I have to tell you something. A lot of things happened yesterday while you were at school. Andi is a detective out of Dallas. She got into a bit of trouble by being in the wrong place at the wrong time. And now she thinks she's being stalked. The sheriff and Dan are helping her out. Once she testifies, trouble will be over. Pecos thought it best if she lays low here in Honey Creek tonight. I offered her my apartment last night. Dan is on guard with her. They left at dawn; they're already gone. The sheriff, Dan, and Bear have a plan to get her out of town."

Noah smiled. "I'm part of the team. Everyone calls into me." He straightened. "I think they call that Central Command."

Cora sat up and cuddled against his side. "Tell me all the details."

Noah smiled. "I'll tell you everything tonight, but right now I want to hold you before you have to leave. School all day then you have PTA. I might not see you for twelve hours."

"You've lived thirty-three years without me."

Noah shut his eyes. "Wrong, I didn't start living until I saw you."

Two hours after his mother woke him up, Noah stood on the landing and kissed Cora goodbye. "One more, one more," he pleaded.

"You're going to kiss my lips off," she said with a smile. "What a morning. What a way to start the day."

She turned to head to school, and he stepped into his bookshop. In his mind's eye he could already see a huge desk in the corner near the windows, out of the way and waiting for him to write.

They say that one person out of a hundred who wants to be

a writer actually finds success. He stood tall like a matador, ready for the fight. Once he got the desk downstairs, he'd write *I'm the one. I'm the writer* in five-inch letters above where he sat.

He might not ever be his mother's son again, but he was his own man as of today.

The morning passed with no word from the sheriff or Dan. He'd heard footsteps in the apartment much earlier, and he heard they'd left for Holly Rim at dawn. She must be safe by now. He could stop worrying and think about a story that he birthed from pieces of the puzzle playing out in this danger and helping others survive.

Suddenly, he laughed. This was the perfect town to write in. He was sure half the people here wanted to write. The other half were crazy and would make great characters.

Noah strolled to the front of the store just as his phone rang. The plan to save Andi was in place. Everyone must be ready. Andi and Dan were at Eliza's Holly Rim, the sheriff was in his office with all his men ready to head out, Rusty and Zach were along the road halfway to Eliza's farm, ready to drive in any direction needed.

Noah was about to wait on his only customer when the phone rang again a few minutes later. He answered on the second ring.

Bear didn't bother with hello. "Noah!" he screamed. "Get ahold of Andi's brothers and tell them the thugs with guns are hiding out at the bend. Rusty and Zach need to delay them for just a few minutes. They're closest. Do not physically engage. I repeat, Do Not Engage. The perps must have followed Dan and Andi out of town."

"Don't worry." Noah paused. "I'll inform Pecos. He needs to get up there."

Bear answered, "This'll all be over in thirty minutes and everyone will be safe if the plan goes okay."

What else could Noah do? He couldn't leave the shop. Except . . . he could call that Texas Ranger that was hanging around Andi last week.

He frantically dug through a cluttered drawer for the card that Ranger Ramm had given him. He grabbed it and dialed the number.

The Texas Ranger answered on the first ring. He wanted facts fast and didn't bother with goodbye. Noah hoped they'd all get there in time.

Chapter 28

Slowing Down Trouble

Rusty threw his truck in gear and raced toward the bend. The pickup's accelerator screeched in protest as he floored it. "I put this thing back together once. We may have to do it again."

"Where are we going?" Zach yelled.

"To the bend, three miles from the rim. Andi's at the ranch out there, and Noah just called to tell us we've got to slow down the guys gunning for her. The sheriff needs more time to get there."

"Don't we need guns or something?"

"No, we're going to use our wits."

Confusion colored Zach's gray eyes. "We got some of those? I don't know about you, but I don't know where mine are."

Rusty glanced over at his little brother to reassure the kid and almost smashed into a mailbox on the side of the road. An idea took hold of him. "Hey, why don't we just hit them?"

"With what?"

"With the truck."

"What will we do after we hit them? I don't think they'd like that."

"We run." It wasn't the best plan Rusty had ever come up with but it would have to do. They had to save their sister.

Half a mile up the road the brothers caught sight of a black Ford almost hidden behind a pile of windblown tumbleweeds.

"You think that's them?" Zach pointed to the group of men standing around the back of the car.

"Of course it is. Old dirt road. Suspicious group of men digging in the trunk of a black vehicle."

"Are you sure?" Zach asked as the men pulled out what looked like assault rifles.

Adrenaline coursed through Rusty. "Yep. We've got them."

The shooters turned as one as the truck kicked up dust, and they dropped their weapons out of sight.

Rusty lowered his voice and glanced at his little brother. "You ever seen a drunk try to drive a pickup?"

"Only a few times." Zach tightened his hands around his seat belt, as if for dear life.

Rusty gripped the wheel harder as his foot smashed on the pedal and he headed straight for the Ford's fender. He grazed the vehicle just enough to slide it back into the mud.

Jumping out of the truck, he told his brother to stay put and staggered toward the men who were looking for his sister. In a slurred voice he said, "I'm sorry, I'm sorry. I thought you were a pole."

Half of the men were cussing and the other half seemed to be yelling death threats at the brothers as they wiped the mud now splattered on their clothes.

Rusty squinted his eyes like he was trying to focus. "Boys, I think you're stuck. But don't you worry, I'll pull you out. I ain't got rope or a chain or anything, but I know where to find some. You just stay put. I'll be back in five."

He stumbled back to his pickup, almost falling into the driver's seat. Then took off before the group even moved.

Out of the silence Zach asked, "Did anyone ever tell you not to run into a gun fight without a gun?"

Smiling, Rusty said, "You don't need a gun when you've got wits." He winked, then added, "And by the way, stop taking pictures and call Noah. Tell him mission accomplished."

Chapter 29

Outrunning Trouble

The women were gazing out at the rim as Bear and Danny brought over their horses. Bear lifted his fairy into her saddle, but he couldn't look at her face.

"Be careful in the pasture. The grass may be slippery from the rain." He put his big hand over her small ones holding the reins. "Stay in the trees if you hear any firing. You'll be safe hidden there. I put a rifle in the scabbard just in case. Remember, you hold my heart."

"And you hold mine." She looked to him with fear in her eyes. "If you die down here, I'll dig two holes. I don't want to be here without you."

Eliza turned her horse to the rim and Bear slapped its rump without another word. It seemed so quiet suddenly, despite the plodding hooves. He watched Danny lift Andi onto her horse and say his goodbyes.

"Come back to me as soon as you can. When it's safe," the deputy told her.

"I can't," she said. "And don't wait for me either."

"I'll always be here waiting, Andi. Whether you choose to come back or not."

Her mount pranced in a circle and Andi seemed to fight to hold on to it.

Bear asked, "You know how to ride, girl?"

She leaned forward, kicking the horse's flank, and shot out to catch up to Eliza. "To the top!" Andi yelled.

"To the top," Eliza answered.

He turned to the big deputy and tried to mask the sorrow in his voice. "They'll be fine. Eliza will get them out. She's been riding all her life."

They watched in silence as their women raced toward the tree line.

"Slow down now, Andi. The holly will rope your horse's hooves," Andi heard Eliza shout from ten feet in front of her.

"This is a maze. How do you know where you're going?"

"There's a tale of a husband and wife who killed each other. They left gold coins to mark their path to the rim." Eliza pointed to a dark lightning mark that had become a shadow up on a rock above them. "That's the opening to the cave."

Before Andi could answer, a shot sounded from below.

"They'll be getting past the lock on the gate by the road," Eliza said, fear in her eyes.

Both women whirled their horses and headed back down, careful to remain hidden in the tree line. They peered through the leaves at Eliza's farm. Both were silent as they saw the men they loved standing, braced apart, waiting for the shooters to approach.

"They have no cover," Andi pointed out. "They're sitting ducks. Once the perps get past the gate, they'll pick our men off easily. They're being fools."

"No, they're determined." Eliza straightened her shoulders. "They're brave. They'll make sure we're safe."

"They're brave fools," Andi said. "But I can't go through the cave. Danny's putting my life before his own. I can't leave him."

Eliza gripped Andi's hand. "Neither can I."

"If we split up, they can't follow us both. And maybe we can get off a few shots before the shooters even get out of their car. That should distract them."

As they started back down the trail, Andi heard the familiar whirring of a helicopter coming in overhead. She swung the horse around and rode directly toward the perps' car. Like a three-screen movie, everything seemed to happen at once. The sheriff and his deputies swung through Eliza's gate going full throttle.

She watched as the shooters tried to scatter, only to find the helicopter lowering and Texas Rangers hanging out of the open side doors, ready to jump. They were fully armed, dressed from head to toe in protective gear. Their police armor similar to what Pecos and his men were wearing.

The perps stepped away from their car with their hands held high, their assault rifles abandoned on the floorboards of their Ford.

Andi's eyes searched for Dan, and she found him wrestling one of the men into the sheriff's car.

She jumped off the horse and ran forward. "Danny!" she called.

He looked up and caught her eye. "I'll meet you at the station," he yelled over the commotion.

Ranger Ramm cut in from behind her. "No, she can't. Andi's coming with me." He turned to Andi. "There's a mole in the department. Someone's been monitoring your emails. The judge pushed up the trial date to keep you safe."

A mole. That explained how they'd found her in this tiny town.

Dan took a step toward her, sorrow in his eyes. "Come back to me."

"I don't know if I can. I don't know when this will all be over." She looked away, hiding the tears filling hers. "And even if I came back for a while, I couldn't stay. You can't clip my wings. I told you, my home is in the clouds."

"Andi, do you love me?"

"Yes, but I can't be tied down."

"Then I'll wait for you."

"For how long, Deputy?"

"For you, honey, I'd wait forever."

As she followed Ramm to the chopper, no one but Andi seemed to notice Eliza ride straight to Bear and jump out of the saddle right into his arms.

Bear's heart swelled as he tightened his arms around his fairy. "You're safe," he said, burying his face in her hair. "You're safe now."

Tears flowed down her cheeks. "I know, but we've lost our secret love. Everyone will know now."

"Maybe. But we'll gain a marriage," Bear said.

Chapter 30

Small Town Paradise

Noah typed *The End* on the last page of his first book. He loved writing. It didn't seem like work at all. And he loved the little corner of his bookstore that was all his. He put his feet up on the old desk he'd moved down from the third floor. Even though he hadn't known it was in the building, he knew the desk had always belonged here and not up there.

He hadn't changed a thing on it. He'd kept the scars and scraps and the missing bottom drawer. It didn't matter. The space was the perfect size for writing his manuscript. In the mornings in the winter, only a few people came into the bookstore. Some days he'd finish a chapter, but most of the time he'd only write a page as he watched his town wake up.

His eyes followed Cora waddling around, tidying up the bookshop. It was the perfect timing. The baby would be here in a few months, and his novel would be published by then. And Noah knew he probably wouldn't have any more time for writing for a while. But it was okay. For once in his life, he was living not just watching.

The bookshop had become like Cora's second home. She

loved rearranging the bookstore, and Noah had a feeling he would be the next project. Every time his new sister-in-law would come in, Katherine would suggest Cora change something about him. Last week she'd been pointing out his hair. This week would probably be his baggy clothes. And Noah didn't even want to hear about her changing his shoes. They'd been good to him for the past five years.

But he just smiled. He knew Cora didn't care about his clothes. She loved him. And he didn't mind his bugging sister-in-law. She just made his wife look more perfect.

Bear had torn out the walls of the three small apartments on the second floor of the mall and built them a space as big as a house, with windows facing Main and the town square and on the other side a quiet creek.

Katherine had decided it was her place to decorate the baby's room. After all, she claimed she knew how to decorate, even if she didn't really know what a baby would need. Eliza had painted a wall in the baby's room with the characters from her favorite children's books. Soon, they'd all be ready for the new arrival.

Noah smiled, imagining Bear as a grandfather. He knew his father-in-law would do great. Somehow Eliza had tamed the wild man. He'd even brought out his old suit for his youngest daughter's wedding. Noah laughed as he remembered Bear saying that he'd bought it years ago for Katherine's first marriage and worn it to every one since. But after Cora's wedding, he was going to retire it.

Bear had told Noah after the arrests at Eliza's farm that he'd seen the way Noah couldn't seem to let go of Cora, even hours after the excitement was over. Noah remembered Bear standing up, pointing his fingers, and saying, "Marry my daughter." And all Noah could say was "I plan to."

Cora's only answer had been a kiss on Noah's cheek and a smile. Bear would know she'd already said yes.

Noah was watching the town let go of winter. The sun was shining and the Over the Hill walkers were restarting their circuit. He noticed their jogging suits were a little tight now. Eggnog and cookies in the winter and coffee and jogging the square in spring. The cycle was repeating.

He spotted Eliza's pickup parked outside Bear's shop and smiled. More and more she was coming into Honey Creek these days. She was slowly becoming part of their family and part of the town.

Once, one of the walkers asked her why she hadn't married Bear. And Eliza had smiled and said, "He's always been mine."

Noah turned back to his desk and thought about how he'd run away from his parents and New York, and everyone thinking he was crazy. Who would have guessed that in this little town in the middle of Texas he would have found the love of his life? He knew, like many of the people in Honey Creek, he'd be happy here with Cora by his side. He didn't need adventure or excitement. He wanted his life to read like a great book, one when you finished the last page, the story was complete.

Chapter 31

Flying Home

Danny Davis sat alone on his horse on the tallest hill overlooking his family farm. In the distance, he could see his dream house. It was almost finished, no longer just a frame against the sky. From the outside it looked complete. All it needed now was some paint and a picket fence. The almost home looked lonely, but soon he hoped it would be as full as he envisioned.

He waited in the stillness of the cold day. A part of him felt the land was sleeping. But soon, it would wake. He hated the yellow, dead grass and the bare trees, but he knew it would come alive again. A hawk drifted by on the wind, as if looking for winter to leave.

Spring would be here soon. The world was turning. But winter still clung to the breeze. He watched the sky, thinking of Andi. Remembering every moment they'd spent together. The times they'd fought, the times they'd kissed, the times they'd battled their way out of trouble.

Some mornings he could have sworn she was lying beside him. She'd felt just right snuggled against his side. Dreaming of Andi was better than ever touching another.

He'd taken down the little picture of Karly from his closet.

He thought back on that first love as just a creek, but loving Andi was like a powerful rapid washing over him. Danny didn't have a picture of Andi to replace it with, but he saw her always in his mind. The long blond hair spilled over his pillow. Her perfect body moving bare in the moonlight.

He loved her fire. Andi was all-out in her life, and he was still drifting through his.

His flannel shirt that she'd worn hung on a hook by the doorframe so it was the first thing he saw when he awoke and the last thing he saw when he went to bed. He could still smell her. He balled his fist in the flannel. All he had of her were memories. How could someone come into his life for a little over a week and change his dreams? He still wanted his someday house, he still wanted his career, but his life would be hollow until Andi returned.

There were a thousand reasons why he loved her, but he couldn't think of a single one for her to come back to him. He felt like he needed her to breathe. And he knew she loved him, but she was so independent. She could go on without him in her life.

They rarely talked on the phone since she'd left for the trial. She was busy wrapping up the investigation. But when she did call, Dan's world stopped for a few minutes and he remembered. He told himself over and over that she'd come back someday because every time he said goodbye, he sensed a whisper of her need for him to calm her world.

Dan yelled over the clouds for her to come home every time he rode up on this hill, waiting. He'd meant it when he said he'd wait for her forever. He'd thought many times to get in his pickup and go to her in Dallas. But that was her world and he couldn't just step in.

The roar of a Cessna sounded in the distance. It grew louder, like it was coming toward him. He didn't breathe as hope sprung up in him. Then he saw the plane.

Andi.

214 / *Jodi Thomas*

She was circling, and he was waving. The engines slowed as she lowered and finally landed on a brand-new air strip he'd built on over a half acre as if she'd landed there a dozen times before.

Danny rode to the end of the strip as Andi navigated down the runway that was shiny and new. He grinned as if she was wearing a wedding dress and this was the day they were going to be joined.

As the plane came to a stop, he kicked his horse into motion and raced to where she was rolling in. When she opened the cockpit door, Dan was there to catch her as she flew toward him.

He whirled her around. "How long are you home?" he whispered as he hugged her against his heart.

"A few days. Then I've got to go back to Dallas one last time."

Laughing, Andi attacked him with kisses. Danny didn't try to defend himself at all.

"I don't care where you go or where you have to fly to as long as you come home to me," he said.

As he let her down, she danced around the runway. "I can't believe you built this. You really must love me because ranchers and farmers never give up their land."

"I'll love you forever, honey." He smiled. "I won't clip your wings. You can always leave. Just come back."

"Not this time. But soon. One day, when I fly in, I plan to stay. You are my home, Danny. No matter where I go, I'll always come home." She smiled, love burning in her eyes.

"To the land?"

"No. To your arms."

Coming soon . . .

Jodi Thomas's
SILVERLEAF RAPIDS
A Ransom Canyon novel
The prequel to the *New York Times* bestselling Ransom
Canyon series!
Soon to be a Netflix series!

Look for it in late 2024 . . .

Visit our website at
KensingtonBooks.com
to sign up for our newsletters, read
more from your favorite authors, see
books by series, view reading group
guides, and more!

Become a Part of Our
Between the Chapters Book Club
Community and Join the Conversation